THE GHOST FILES

Haunted High Book 2

The Ghost Files

By Cheree Alsop

ISBN:1979712999
Cover Design by Robert Emerson
Editing by Sue Player
www.ChereeAlsop.com

To my husband Michael,
The love of my life who shares the rush of
Riding motorcycles, traveling to distant shores,
And the joy of reaching our dreams.

To my children, Myree, Aiden, and Ashton,
Anything you dream is possible.
Always believe.

ALSO BY CHEREE ALSOP

The Haunted High Series-
The Wolf Within Me
The Ghost Files
City of Demons

The Silver Series-
Silver
Black
Crimson
Violet
Azure
Hunter
Silver Moon

The Werewolf Academy Series-
Book One: Strays
Book Two: Hunted
Book Three: Instinct
Book Four: Taken
Book Five: Lost
Book Six: Vengeance
Book Seven: Chosen

Heart of the Wolf Part One
Heart of the Wolf Part Two

The Galdoni Series-
Galdoni
Galdoni 2: Into the Storm
Galdoni 3: Out of Darkness

The Small Town Superheroes Series-
Small Town Superhero
Small Town Superhero II
Small Town Superhero III

Keeper of the Wolves
Stolen
The Million Dollar Gift
Thief Prince
When Death Loved an Angel

The Shadows Series
Shadows- Book One in the World of Shadows
Mist- Book Two in the World of Shadows

The Monster Asylum Series
Book One- The Fangs of Bloodhaven
Book Two- The Scales of Drakenfall

Girl from the Stars
Book 1- Daybreak
Book 2- Daylight
Book 3- Day's End
Book 4- Day's Journey
Book 5- Day's Hunt

The Dr. Wolf Series
Book 1- Shockwave
Book 2- Demon Spiral
Book 3- The Four Horsemen
Book 4- Dragon's Bayne

The Pirate from the Stars
The Prince of Ash and Blood

Chapter One

I KNEW IT WAS A DREAM but couldn't force my eyes to open. I held the demon down, but it struggled, slicing my arms with its claws. I knew if I let it go, it would attack the students around me. When the fire spilled from its mouth and over my hands, it took all of my strength to hold on. Sparrow, my little sylph dragon, used her own fire to protect my left hand, but I could feel the skin on my right one melting away. I couldn't hold on any longer.

A stake made from one of the Academy's banisters skewered the creature through the chest, pinning it to the floor. I was pulled backwards and watched my teammates contain the demon's fire. It spat out one word before it died. *Chutka.*

My eyes opened. I found myself on a bed in the infirmary. Professor Brigg's cloak was still over me where he had laid it when he visited me and found that I was cold. The lights were out and the only sound came from the monitor across from me. The other beds were empty except for one. Claria Fig slept on a bed against the other wall. In order to help her recover from the wounds she had received from the demon, Dr. Six had induced what she called a crystal-maintained slumber to promote faster healing. I thought I was the only one awake until movement caught the corner of my eye.

A figure stood in the far shadows checking supplies on the counter.

"Dr. Six?" I said.

I realized my mistake before the person turned around.

Dr. Six was a short, rotund witch who healed using crystals along with the regular practices I recognized from the normal world. She wore a top hat with strange spectacles on it that looked as though they belonged in some different era.

The person who met my gaze, however, was tall and slender. He was a gentleman I had never seen at the Academy. He wore a black suit with a pristine white shirt except for a hole over the heart that showed dark blood. My heartbeat slowed when the window behind him lit the man in an otherworldly radiance. He opened his mouth and his fangs glowed in the moonlight.

I made the mistake of using my right hand to push up from the bed. The bandages that Dr. Six had wrapped loosely around the burns from the demon fire did little to stop the pain of using it. I gasped and pulled my hand to my chest. When I looked up again, the ghost was right in front of me. I jerked back, causing the sylph dragon who had been sleeping around my left wrist to awaken.

The ghost's eyebrows lifted at my reaction, but he didn't say anything.

10

I figured it was rude to stay silent, so I cleared my throat and said, "S-sorry. I thought I was dreaming."

The man adjusted his glasses with a pale hand and said in a low voice, "Stop dreaming, Mr. Brigs-Bris...." He coughed, then said, "Mr. Briscoe. The demons are restless and the fate of this school is in your hands. The ghost of your heart holds the key. Lock the door or all is lost."

The ghost's face changed. The simple, calm expression was taken over by menace. Green flames danced in his yellow eyes and he bared his fangs. A hiss escaped him as he lunged forward, aiming for my throat. I let out a yell and backed up. I fell off the bed and made the mistake of putting my hand down to brace my fall. Pain jolted up my arm as the ghost lunged again. I raised my left arm to shield my face from its touch.

Sparrow lifted her head and hissed at the creature. The sound was surprisingly loud coming from such a little dragon. The ghost jerked back. Sparrow hissed again and a puff of mint-scented blue flame flickered from her mouth.

The ghost glared at me. "You won't always have friends to protect you, *Wolvenbracker*."

Footsteps sounded in the hallway. The ghost looked over his shoulder, then vanished.

Alden burst through the door. "Finn?" he called.

"Over here," I replied as I pushed gingerly to my feet. My knees shook, so I leaned against the bed for support.

"What happened?" Alden asked, his eyes wide.

I shook my head, not sure where to start. Sparrow ran up my arm and sat on my shoulder. Her little claws kneaded my tee-shirt in agitation. I ran the fingers of my good hand over her back.

"We saw a ghost," I told the Grim.

"I knew it!" Alden said beneath his breath.

I was about to describe the ghost when his words stopped me. "How did you know?" I asked.

He lowered his head so that his face was hidden by his unruly straight white hair and he said, "I felt creepy-crawly." He glanced up at me and continued with, "It sounds stupid, I know, but my mom always described it that way, so I knew there had to be a ghost here somewhere." Embarrassment showed on his face when he said, "At least, I hoped so."

"Why?" I asked, baffled as to why anyone would want to see a ghost, especially after what I had encountered.

Alden gave me an apologetic smile. "Because that means I'll be good at my job."

I didn't know what to say to my friend whose job would eventually be to escort those who had died to whatever lay beyond.

I must have appeared a bit lost, because he said, "So, uh, why were you on the floor?"

That jolted me back to the present. "We need to get the team together."

"Right now?" Alden asked, surprised.

I nodded. "Right now, and probably as many professors as we can get. We have a serious problem." Before he could leave the room, the thought that was swirling in my mind had to be addressed. "Alden, one more thing?"

The Grim turned with an expectant look. "What?"

"I need you to find out whatever you can about a demon named Chutka. I have a feeling he's got something to do with what's going on here."

"I start researching," the Grim replied with an air of pride as if having the job was important to him.

"Thanks. And let's keep it on the downlow," I suggested. "We don't want to alarm anyone."

"Good idea," Alden agreed.

12

He took off out the door and left me to make my way to the meeting room.

I was surprised to hear voices coming from the hidden room beyond the secret passage when I reached it. I had figured that leaving when Alden did would give me a head start, but given everything that happened the night before, my pace was much slower than I had intended. By the time I reached the door, I had to lean against it to catch my breath.

I heard voices coming up behind me.

"Are you sure Finn-wolf wasn't hallucinating? Yesterday was pretty stressful," Lyris said with concern in her voice.

"Ghosts are no joke," Brack's booming voice echoed through the corridor.

"Finn's not hallucinating or joking," Alden replied. "I felt them, too."

"Great, now you're both ghosted," Dara muttered.

They appeared around the corner as Alden asked, "What's ghosted?"

"Ironic, coming from a Grim," she pointed out.

"It means being haunted," Lyris replied. The beam of her flashlight swept across my face and she gave a little shriek. The other lights followed hers. The witch's expression showed her embarrassment when she met my gaze. "S-sorry, Finn. Your eyes shone gold in the light. I thought you were, well...."

"A monster?" I suggested.

That brought a little laugh from her and the others as they hurried to reach me. "Yeah," she said.

"You were right," I replied with a smile.

Brack patted my shoulder hard enough to nearly knock me over. "Good to see you, buddy," he said.

"How's your hand?" Lyris asked.

"It hurts," Dara and I said at the same time.

13

I shook off the hand she had set on my arm. "I'm fine," I told her.

The empath didn't believe me. "You should be sleeping."

"I was sleeping," I replied. "It's not my fault a ghost tried to bite me."

"Ghosts don't bite," a voice said from the other end of the hallway. "I bite."

Vicken held the flashlight to his face as he drew near. The light illuminated his fangs. The two vampires behind him did the same.

"Knock it off," Lyris scolded. "Finn doesn't need anything else to be scared of tonight."

"I wasn't scared!" I protested.

Everyone looked at Alden.

He shrugged uncomfortably. "You did fall off your bed," he replied quietly.

"You told them that?" I asked. I shook my head. "You try being attacked by a ghost. It's not as fun as it sounds."

"It doesn't sound fun," Brack replied solemnly.

All joking left Vicken and he said, "Now that you're up, we can continue searching for Amryn."

"He should be sleeping," Dara told the vampire.

"He promised to find my sister," Vicken replied.

"He could have died back there!" Lyris argued. "He nearly lost his hands!"

"Until I shoved a stake through the demon's chest," Vicken pointed out.

With half-amusement and half-annoyance, I listened to them argue about what I was supposed to do until I heard Alden mutter, "Ironic, a vampire staking someone else."

Vicken grabbed the Grim by the front of his shirt. "What did you say?" he demanded.

In an attempt to break the vampire's hold on my friend, I grabbed his arm with my right hand without thinking. I

14

sucked in a breath at the pain and let go. I cradled my arm against my chest and leaned against the door.

"Look what you guys did," Dara said.

"I'm fine," I told them.

Vicken set Alden down and silence filled the small tunnel.

The door opened. I would have fallen backwards if Vicken hadn't grabbed my good hand with the lightning-quick reflexes of a vampire.

"Are you going to stand out there all night and argue, or come in here and tell us why we all got dragged out of bed?" Professor Briggs demanded.

Vicken let me go and motioned for me to enter first. The wolf in me fought against turning my back on the vampire. I took a steeling breath and did so anyway with the knowledge that if the vampire did choose to attack me in front of the professors, at least he would get expelled. It wasn't the most reassuring thought I'd had, but I would hold onto anything at that point.

Headmistress Wrengold met me at the couch. "How are you feeling, Mr. Briscoe?" she asked.

"Better," I replied, going with the easy answer.

I handed Professor Briggs the cloak he had let me borrow. He took it with a searching look. "Are you alright?" he asked quietly.

I nodded. "I'm better than I was."

"You need more rest," Professor Mellon said. My Creature Languages teacher motioned toward the couch with a kind smile. "Sit down, Mr. Briscoe. You look like you're going to fall over."

"He already did," I heard Vicken mutter next to me.

I shot the vampire a look.

He held my gaze, his yellow eyes boring into mine. "You promised," he said under his breath for only my ears.

"I keep my promises," I replied.

"What was that?" Mercer asked from his seat on a folding chair near the fireplace. The man's stony expression didn't give away his thoughts.

I shook my head and took a seat. "Nothing," I told the sweeper.

The other students chose seats around the room. The smell of the food on the table made my stomach rumble. I wondered when I had eaten last, and also wondered who made sure the table was always full of food.

After a moment of silence, I realized everyone was watching me.

"You called us here...," Briggs prompted.

"Because a ghost attacked me in the infirmary," I replied, confused because I thought Alden had already told them.

"Ghosts don't attack people," the skeletal professor said.

"If you've just experienced a near-death experience like Finn has, perhaps seeing a ghost attacking you is normal," Professor Mantis pointed out with her long arms folded across her stomach.

I sat up. "I didn't hallucinate it. The ghost was a vampire. He spoke, well, like he was from the past or something, and then his face changed and he attacked me."

Silence filled the room. It was broken by Headmistress Wrengold who asked, "Changed, how?"

I let out a slow breath and described it in the only way I could. "As if a demon possessed him."

That caught their attention.

Professor Briggs asked Mercer, "Can ghosts be possessed by demons?"

Professor Mellon twined a strand of her long red hair anxiously around a finger as she asked Professor Mantis, "Have you ever heard of such a thing? My cats have been restless."

Professor Tripe pushed his blue hair back and said in his monotone voice, "I need to study more on demon psychology. Perhaps his involvement with the demons has gotten into his head."

I glanced at Dara and Lyris. Both of them watched me with something akin to pity on their faces. It ate at me. I stood up and nearly shouted, "I'm not making this up!" Everyone stared at me. I clenched my hands into fists, regardless of how it hurt. "The ghost was in the infirmary when I woke up. It said, 'Stop dreaming, Mr. Briscoe. The demons are restless and the fate of this school is in your hands. The ghost of your heart holds the key. Lock the door or all is lost.' Then its face changed and it tried to bite my neck." I held up my left hand to show them the dragon sleeping soundly around my wrist as if nothing had happened. "Sparrow blew her flame at him and he backed away and said, 'You won't always have friends to protect you, *Wolvenbracker.*'"

I leaned against the arm of the couch with my arms crossed in front of my chest. I had to struggle against the urge to phase. If I turned into wolf form, I would be stuck that way until my body decided to phase back. It wouldn't help my argument at all if I couldn't participate.

"He called you Wolvenbracker?" Briggs said, his quiet voice carrying through the room.

I nodded, grateful someone at least didn't think I was making it up any longer. "What does it mean?"

"It's elvish for wolf threat," the professor answered.

"How did he know I was a werewolf?"

Briggs shook his head. "I have no idea, but I think his warning should be taken seriously enough. 'The demons are restless and the fate of this school is in your hands. The ghost of your heart holds the key. Lock the door or all is lost,'" he

17

recited. He gave me a searching look. "Who is the ghost of your heart?"

Thoughts of Sebastian's death when the car I drove plummeted into the icy river surfaced immediately. I let out a slow breath. "I, uh, I think it means a friend of mine who died."

"How would he hold the key?" Professor Tripe asked. "That makes no sense."

"Neither does a biting ghost," Professor Mellon reminded him. "We're going to have to take this one step at a time." She thought for a moment, then said, "The demons are restless. That, we already know thanks to your team's encounter with the one in the corridor." She tipped her head in gratitude toward the students who waited with me. "What about the door? If we can't find the door, the key is useless. We need to find out where the demons are coming from."

"They must be using an object to let themselves into our world, something from here but not of here," Professor Briggs said.

"How do we find it?" Vicken asked.

In his face showed the hope that whatever this key was, it would lead us to his sister.

"I'm not sure," Headmistress Wrengold answered. "But we know that your sister is missing and have reason to think the demons are at fault."

It surprised me when she met my gaze. I nodded, wondering who had told her that I had smelled demons in Amryn's room.

"We also know that parents are coming in two days," she continued. "We have a lot to address with them, all things considered."

That was news to me. I raised my hand.

"You don't have to raise your hand," Vicken said with a roll of his eyes.

I ignored him. "Are all parents coming?"

The Headmistress nodded. "I emailed all of the parents last night. With the demon attack and the continued threat, we felt that...."

Her voice faded away from my attention at the thought of Dad, Julianne, and Drake visiting Haunted High. As much as I missed my family, I wasn't sure they were ready for something as extreme as vampires and witches, not to mention the tentacled or winged students.

Someone nudged me. I glanced to the right in time to see a strange expression on Alden's face. He rubbed his arms and met my gaze.

"Creepy-crawly?" I whispered.

He nodded.

A scent of cinnamon and dew touched my nose. I stood from where I had been leaning against the arm of the couch and looked around the room. The Headmistress' voice quieted as if she had noticed Alden's reaction as well.

A dark form stood on the other side of the fireplace. I had dismissed the darkness as shadow, but as I watched, his form solidified. He wasn't the vampire from earlier; of that I was sure. His shoulders were too wide, I could see that even facing the fire the way he was. He wore a dark suit with tails and a silver chain from his pocket caught in the firelight.

"A ghost," Lyris whispered from her place on the couch.

The ghost turned and his gaze locked on hers. His face was gaunt and the skin hung below his eyes and from his jowls like a hound dog. I heard Lyris give a little squeak of fear.

"Where is my cat?" the ghost asked.

"I-I don't know," Lyris replied.

The ghost took a step forward. Out of the corner of my eye, I saw the professors gather closer to the couch to protect her.

"You stole my cat," the ghost accused.

Lyris shook her head quickly. "I-I didn't, honest. I would never steal a cat."

"You lie!" the ghost said, crossing closer to where Lyris cringed against Dara.

I placed myself between the ghost and Lyris. His eyes flicked to mine and narrowed. I felt Sparrow let go of my wrist and climb up to my shoulder.

"Heathen," he breathed. "How dare you steal Minkylou."

"I didn't take her," I said. "But you need to back off. You're scaring my friend."

Green flames flickered to life in his gaze. His face twisted the way the vampire's had. He lifted his arms and lunged at me.

Sparrow breathed out her blue flame. It hit the ghost in the face. He gasped and clawed at his eyes, vanishing as he did so.

The Headmistress broke the shocked silence. "Did the other ghost's face change like that?"

I nodded.

Mercer's rough voice grated from his place on the other side of the fire. "If demons are inhabiting ghosts in order to breech the Academy, we have a serious problem."

The Headmistress let out a breath and said, "We can only hope Alden's parents can handle the ghost situation before the parents arrive."

Everyone looked at Alden.

He nodded quickly. "They're the best with ghosts. Trust me."

"These aren't normal ghosts," Briggs said so quietly I suspected he pitched it for only me to hear.

"Luckily, we're not normal students," I replied.

20

Chapter Two

"GHOSTS ARE EVERYWHRE. THIS is a disaster," Mrs. Hassleton said as she hurried to answer the door for the first of the parents.

"At least they aren't attacking people," Alden said under his breath.

I knew he was defensive of how hard his parents had worked to try to banish the ghosts, but since nobody knew the reason they were there, the Grims were having a hard time sending them back.

A ghost floated past as we spoke. The slightly glowing, transparent girl studied the book in her hand and floated through several students as if she didn't notice them. The students she touched hurried out of her path. The ghost floated into the wall and vanished from sight.

Despite numerous frights, the ghosts hadn't attacked anyone since our confrontation in the hidden room. Most of them drifted around as if they didn't see our world. Those who did stayed as much out of the students' way as we did of them. Except for one who had attempted to teach Professor Tripe's Mythical Creature Anatomy class, the ghosts remained fairly innocuous.

"Are you worried about what your dad will think of the ghosts?" Alden asked when he glanced at my face.

I let out the breath I had been holding without realizing it. "Among everything else. Dad's open to this whole idea, but I have no clue how much my mom told him." I looked away from Alden's knowing gaze when I admitted, "If it's as much as she told me about being a werewolf, that adds up to nothing."

Alden gave me a reassuring smile. "Don't worry," he said. "He let you come here knowing his son would be the first werewolf at Haunted High in twenty-five years. He knows you need to be here for a reason; I'll bet he comes with an open mind."

I would have accepted his words if I hadn't read Julianne's text the night before. Dad had snuck me a cellphone before he left so we could keep in touch. Our brief conversations, if you could call them that, had at least lessened the feeling of homesickness enough for me to stick it out at the Academy. But I worried about my stepmother, Julianne. She was seven months pregnant and didn't need the stress of learning what other kind of monsters lived in our world.

EXCITED TO COME SEE YOU TOMORROW. I MADE YOUR FAVORITE STROGANOFF EVEN THOUGH YOUR DAD SAYS BRINGING FOOD MIGHT NOT BE THE BEST IDEA GIVEN THE OTHER

STUDENTS. DO YOU KNOW WHAT HE MEANS BY THAT?- JULI (followed by the inevitable flower and smiley face).

I had written back, *THERE'S A LOT OF HUGE APPETITES HERE. THEY ARE STRICT ABOUT NO FOOD LEAVING THE CAFETERIA. I THINK THEY'RE WORRIED ABOUT RATS.- FINN*

I couldn't decide if that made things better or worse. If Julianne showed up worried about huge rodents only to realize that there were students here who looked like rodents, she might have the baby right there in the corridor. I was pretty sure that hadn't happened before at Haunted High.

"Welcome to The Remus Academy for Integral Education," Mrs. Hassleton said as she pulled open the door.

I wondered briefly why she had to open it. When Dad and I had first reached the Academy a week ago, the door had swung open on its own. Apparently, that wasn't normal. I made a mental note to ask about it later.

My train of thought was derailed by the sweeping presence of a vampire who could only be Vicken's father, Don Ruvine, the leader of the national vampire coven.

"Welcome, welcome," Mrs. Hassleton said with only a slight tremor in her voice.

"Thank you, Madame," the vampire replied.

Mrs. Hassleton blushed bright enough to match the pink dress she had worn for parent night.

Don Ruvine crossed to Vicken. Vicken bowed to his father. The Don answered with a single nod.

"Have the Maes sent demands for Mother?" Vicken asked in a voice quiet enough that it strained my wolven hearing.

"Nothing, as of yet," the Don replied in a tone that told how upset he was. "Any word of your sister?"

"No," Vicken replied. He lowered his head. "I'm sorry. We're doing everything we can. It's just—"

His head jerked up and he met my gaze. His eyes narrowed and he gestured toward the cafeteria.

"Let's go somewhere we are less likely to be overheard," he said.

His father's yellow gaze followed his son's. I looked down before he could make eye contact. Relief filled me when their footsteps led away from the busy room.

Other parents entered after the Don. Warlocks and witches were followed by tentacled parents who matched their tentacled students. I smiled when I saw the parents of Adalia from my Creature Languages class. They had her same cat eyes.

"My parents should be down soon," Alden said with a hint of anxiety in his voice. "They said they were performing a sweep of the roof due to a sighting there."

"I know the Headmistress is grateful for all they've done," I told him. "This ghost situation has certainly thrown everyone off."

An ancient looking woman with a cane and a ghostly glow made her way from one end of the corridor to the other. Students stepped away from her faint outline and continued their conversations, though their parents stared at the apparition.

"...it swung open by itself," I heard a familiar voice explain.

A smile crossed my face despite my trepidation.

"Welcome, Mr. Briscoe."

"Thank you," my father told Mrs. Hassleton. "This is my other son, Drake."

"Pleased to meet you," Drake said. He held out his hand.

Mrs. Hassleton gave my father a worried look. "And is he another, um...."

Dad lifted a shoulder. "We're not sure yet. Only time will tell." He squeezed Drake's shoulder and my brother lowered his hand. "But if so, we'll be knocking on your door again."

Mrs. Hassleton gave a strained laugh and turned away.

I saw Drake's eyes widen and followed his gaze to Aerlis and his parents who had the same matching orange horns and orange eyes, though his father's horns were much bigger than the student's, making his hug a careful one. I watched as my brother's gaze left Aerlis and lingered on one of the tentacled families, then flicked to where Jeppy talked animatedly with his family. His purple hair and black eyes appeared to be a mixture of his mother's long plum-colored locks and his father's pupilless black eyes. His dad's equally black skin and dark clothes gave him a solemn appearance. That impression vanished immediately when the man smiled with a youthful grin that made even Alden's enthusiasm pale in comparison.

"Over here!" I called, lifting a hand.

Relief washed over Dad's face as he hurried to meet me.

"You could have mentioned a lot more in your texts," he said, his eyes wide as he stared around.

"I didn't want to scare you," I replied only half-joking. "Where's Julianne?"

Dad gave me an apologetic look. "She's been sick in bed. She said to give you her love and say that apparently morning sickness doesn't strike only in the morning, and sometimes likes to hit hard again during the last trimester. She did send some stroganoff."

He was about to pull it out of the bag he carried, but my warning about enormous appetites wasn't made up.

"I'll, uh, have some later," I said, taking the bag from him.

He winked. "Want to keep it to yourself, huh? It'll make for a good snack when no one's around."

"Is this a ghost?"

I turned to see Drake staring at a boy about my age. His outline was faint and his feet drifted a few inches above the ground. But instead of floating past with eyes that saw a different world than we did, the ghost's gaze was locked on my brother.

"That's a ghost," I said warily. I watched the boy's eyes for any sign of a green flame.

"H-hi," Drake said. He gave a little wave.

"You don't look like Mr. Snederin," the boy said.

Drake glanced at me and then back at the ghost. "I-I'm not," he said. "My name is Drake Briscoe. I'm just visiting."

The boy shook his head. "We aren't allowed to have visitors. You'll get us in trouble."

I saw it then. The green flame flickered to life in the depths of the boy's eyes.

I set my bandaged hand on Drake's shoulder. "Back up," I said quietly.

"I'm just having a talk with a ghost," Drake said as if amused by the thought. "Don't you do that?"

"No," I replied, keeping my eyes locked on the boy. "It doesn't seem to end well."

Drake glanced at me. Out of the corner of my eye, I saw his face pale at the realization of how serious I was.

"Stand behind me," I told him.

To my relief, Drake and my father both obeyed.

"You need to go back to the door," I told the ghost.

"But if I lead visitors to the door, Chutka the Shambler will make me pay," he replied.

I was aware of conversations falling silent around us. Several of the adults appeared to recognize the name. I knew I held the ghost's attention by a small thread. If it broke and the demon took over, the Headmistress' fear of the parents being involved with our problems would come true.

"No one will follow you to the door," I said. I didn't lie. Though I desperately wanted to find the door, I wasn't about to put lives at risk to do so. My best course of action was to convince the ghost to leave in peace.

"How do you know?" he replied.

"Well, I...." I searched for something to say. "I'm a warlock," I continued. "And I can't lie. It's my affinity."

The boy nodded as if my answer was entirely reasonable. "So no one will follow me to the door?"

"That's right," I said in my most calming tone. I wished I could imitate Professor Mellon's calm cadence. I gave my best effort and continued with, "I think the best thing you could do right now is to return to the door and not come back."

The boy stood silently as if considering it. Finally, he nodded and turned away. I watched him cross the room between inhabitants who backed up at his advance. When he finally walked through the wall, I let out the breath I had been holding.

"That was amazing," Drake said. "I can't believe I just saw a ghost. Why did you lie to it and say you were some sort of warlock?"

My gaze flickered to Alden. The Grim's wide eyes said he had also seen the green flames. I forced a smile and turned back to my brother.

"Sometimes ghosts don't want to leave. I had to get him to trust me in order for him to go in peace. It's a ghost thing," I replied. I hoped he would believe me.

"That's cool," he said with a shrug. "I guess you don't want ghosts interfering with learning and all that."

I nodded. "Exactly."

My dad shook his head with an amazed expression. "This place is definitely more than I expected." His brow furrowed. "What happened to your hand?"

I thought at first he was referring to the dragon. I had worn a long-sleeved shirt to hide the creature because I was afraid of overwhelming my family. Something like Sparrow might just push them over the edge. Then I realized he was looking at my right hand. I lifted it.

"Oh, I burned it by accident, in, uh…."

Alden was suddenly at my side. "In shop class," he said. He gave my dad an innocent smile and pushed his white hair back from his forehead. "The professor said it's healing, though."

"Oh, that's good," Dad replied.

I gave Alden a grateful smile. "Dad, this is Alden. We're roommates."

"You have to share a room?" Drake said in dismay.

I nodded. "It's not that bad. Alden's a good roommate."

The Grim beamed at the compliment.

"Pleased to meet you, Alden," my dad said.

"You also, Sir. Finn's told me a lot about you," Alden replied.

Dad held up his hand to show his bandaged thumb. "Then I'll bet he told you being accident prone runs in the family. I did this building our deck."

I laughed. "I can't wait to see it. Is Drake helping?"

Drake shook his head and waved his hands behind Dad as if hoping I wouldn't go there.

"Not exactly," Dad said.

"Why? Is the younger weremutt as useless as my boy says this one is?"

My blood ran cold at the sound of Don Ruvine's voice behind me. A tremor ran though my skin and my instincts warned that I should never let a vampire sneak up on me. I closed my hands into fists and used the pain of my burned palm to keep the wolf from surfacing.

"You shouldn't talk to my son like that," Dad said, his eyes narrowing.

I put a hand on his chest to keep him from advancing toward the vampire. "Dad, it's okay. Vampires don't like werewolves."

Dad shook his head, his gaze not leaving the vampire. "It's not okay. He shouldn't talk about you like that."

"Takes a weremutt to defend another weremutt," Don Ruvine growled.

I looked to Vicken for help. He shook his head from his place behind his dad and lifted his hands as if to say he couldn't interfere. The irony that it was the same gesture Drake had made about the deck only made me more frustrated.

"What is your problem?" Dad demanded.

Don Ruvine took another step forward. "That they allowed a werewolf back here after what happened before," he spat. "If they won't take care of the problem, maybe I will."

"You'll have to go through me, first," Dad said.

He attempted to move me out of the way, but my werewolf strength gave me an advantage.

"Glad to, weremutt," Don Ruvine replied.

I shoved the vampire back with a strength that surprised him as much as me by his expression. He stumbled back and then surged forward with hatred on his face.

"My dad's human," I said before he could reach us.

My words echoed around the suddenly quiet room.

Don Ruvine stopped as if he had hit a wall. He looked from me to my father in shock. I don't know if he regarded my dad's presence in the middle of a room full of monsters as bravery or stupidity, but after a moment of silence, he shook his head and stalked away.

"Come on, Vicken. This place has truly gone to the dogs," I heard him say before they left the corridor.

Talking returned, though not with the casualness of before.

"Well that was rude," Dad said.

I shook my head, careful to keep my voice low. We didn't need to attract more attention than we already had. "There's a lot of prejudice here." I held Dad's gaze. "It apparently started with the uncle I never knew existed."

"You know about Uncle Mark," Drake pointed out.

"Not Uncle Mark," I replied, keeping my eyes on Dad. "I'm talking about Uncle Conrad, the werewolf who tore this place apart and killed innocent people. That's why werewolves haven't been allowed in this school for twenty-five years. Mom's brother was a murderer."

Dad's lowered gaze told me he had known about Conrad. He sighed and I heard the heaviness of years of keeping my mother's secret. "I hoped it wouldn't affect you."

"Don Ruvine was there, Dad," I replied. "My professor's girlfriend was killed along with the Headmaster, and others they won't even tell me about. It was bad, really bad."

He gave me a tight-lipped smile and set a hand on my shoulder. "I knew that if anyone could turn the view of werewolves around, it was you."

I blew out a breath and shook my head. "I don't think I can do that, but it would have been nice to know what I was getting into."

"I'm sorry, Finn," he said with true heaviness in his voice. "I should have told you instead of letting you find out this way."

I heard footsteps behind me.

"Not everyone at the Academy is as prejudiced as the Don," Alden's father said.

I turned and gave him a grateful smile. "I appreciate you letting your son be my friend."

Alden's mother gave her son a fond look. "We know better than to tell Alden who to befriend; but we would have recommended a werewolf had we known one resided at the Academy."

His father nodded. "A friendship with a werewolf is a lasting one as long as you stay true to it."

That made me smile. "Someone told me the same thing about Grims," I said, thinking back to a conversation I'd had with Professor Briggs.

Mr. Grim nodded. "Whoever told you that was wise."

Alden's mother smiled. "We were friends with your mother when she came to this school."

"Did you know that?" I asked Alden in surprise.

He shook his head quickly. "I had no idea!"

Mr. Grim gave my dad a warm look. "Such true friendships must come naturally."

My father held out his hand. "I agree. It's an honor to meet a friend of Silvia's."

Mr. Grim looked surprised at my dad's gesture. He took the hand and shook it heartily as if he hadn't had a proper handshake in years. I caught a glimpse of the names that glowed on the Grim's forearm before he let go of Dad's hand and his sleeve slid back down to hide them. "Yes, well, we're just glad her son is rooming with ours. With all these ghosts and demons plaguing the country, we're lucky to have them together."

"Demons?" My dad gave me a searching look. "I thought Headmistress Wrengold's letter was being ironic, not that there were actual demons attacking."

"Oh, it's, uh, it's under control," I replied. "I didn't want to worry you." My hand throbbed as I thought of the fact that my team was the control I mentioned.

Dad continued to watch me. "Just so you're safe," he said.

"I am," I reassured him.

"Don't worry," Mrs. Grim told my dad. "They are safer here inside the Academy than they would be outside of it."

Alden and I exchanged a look of uncertainty that we quickly smothered.

"I'm glad to hear it," my dad replied. He shook his head. "I never had to worry about demons at Finn's last school. Our biggest threat are the Devils from Lincoln."

"You have devils?" Mrs. Grim said in horror. "I'm so sorry!"

Dad realized she was serious and laughed. "They're the neighboring high school; they were one of Finn's biggest competitions in track. Right, Finn?"

I forced a laugh and said, "Right, Dad. They were tough."

"They were until that Ertz kid broke his leg," Drake replied.

I stared at him. "Really? He took the title from me twice!"

"I know," my brother said with a grin. "Now it's my turn to win it!"

I nodded. "You do that. Keep it in the family."

"Always," Drake replied.

"Ghosts," someone said.

I turned, expecting to see the usual specter drifting through the corridor. But instead of one, there were at least a dozen of them. As with the others, they didn't seem to see us or at least ignored our presence. A few were talking in a group and wandering through as if they belonged at the school. I realized with a start that given their age, they may have occupied the school back when my mom was a student.

"They seem content just to be, for now," Mr. Grim said musingly.

"We should stay close by in case things take a turn," his wife suggested.

Mr. Grim nodded with his gaze on the ghosts. "I agree."

"Silvia?"

I glanced back to see my father hurry up the stairs toward the second floor.

When I met Drake's gaze, my brother shrugged. "I don't know what he's up to."

Instinct bade me to follow. "I'll check it out," I said. "Stay with Alden. He'll, uh, keep you safe."

It sounded stupid to say, but I didn't dare leave my brother alone with Don Ruvine stalking about in an apparent search for a fight. Alden nodded in agreement.

"Thanks," I said.

I ran up the stairs after my dad, but he wasn't on the second floor.

"Silvia, wait!" I heard him call from further up the steps.

I took them four at a time and felt a brief amazement at the way my body responded with a strength I had never known. The fact that my werewolf side was becoming more obvious made me nervous. I reached the thirteenth floor and slid to a stop.

"Silvia, it's me, Stephen, your husband," Dad said with pleading in his voice. I could hear him gasping from the exertion of the run, and he leaned with his hands on his knees to catch his breath.

His back was to me. Beyond him, a figure floated down the hallway toward the window at the end. It was the same window I had jumped through to save students from demon fire.

My heart slowed at the sight of the ghost's wavy golden hair. Memories pushed at my mind, beckoning from the photographs in the album on our coffee table and the family videos I had watched over and over until I had them memorized.

I saw her in my mind's eye from the video of when she and my dad had visited the ocean. She stood with the waves lapping gently at her bare feet. Her hair was caught in the light of the sun so that it shone like pure gold, and when she turned, the happiness in her eyes matched the laughter that sounded like music from her lips. It was my favorite video. I had watched it so many times I knew how long it took for her to turn and laugh. Her hand was on her belly, pregnant with me. I guess in a way it had been my first visit to the ocean, too.

"Mom?" I said. The word felt strange coming from my lips. It had been so very long since I had called anyone that.

The ghost turned and the present warred with the video from the ocean. Her golden hair shone with otherworldly light and when she looked at me, I found myself staring into bright green eyes that matched my own.

"Up and around, tickle the troll, find your way down, and pay the toll," she said.

Dad dropped to his knees beside me.

"Mom, I don't know," I began, but she cut me off.

"Up and around, tickle the troll, find your way down, and pay the toll," she said again.

She gave me another warm smile, then turned and floated toward the window.

"Silvia, wait!" Dad called. He stumbled to his feet and ran after her.

I caught his arm to keep him from dashing through the window when she drifted to the other side.

"Dad, stop!" I told him when he struggled to break free.

We both watched Mom stride out into the night as though she was still walking along the hallway. The moonlight illuminated her with a greater glow until she reached the edge of the roof and disappeared.

A whisper broke from my dad's lips. "Silvia."

Chapter Three

DAD SANK DOWN AND I followed. We both sat with our backs against the wall. My heart thundered. I put a hand on my chest, willing it to slow. With the moonlight filtering in above us, it was hard to keep the wolf at bay.

"I don't understand," my dad said in a voice that was weak and sad.

I didn't either, but I could tell that if I didn't give him something to hold onto, he was going to climb out on that roof if it was the last thing he did.

"Ghosts have been showing up at the Academy ever since the demon attacked," I told him. I held up my wrapped hand and admitted, "That's where I got this."

Dad focused on me for the first time since I had reached the thirteenth floor. "I thought you got that in class."

I shook my head. "I just didn't want you to worry." I sighed and admitted, "I guess we're far past that, now. When the demon attacked, I helped fight it and we were able to kill it, but the professors think the demon's presence means a doorway has been opened."

I didn't want to tell them that a ghost had actually told me that before it attacked me. The last thing he needed to know was that there were volatile ghosts along with the image of my mother.

I grasped onto that thought. "The Grims, Alden's parents, have been trying to send the ghosts back to where they came from, but they've been struggling because they say most of these aren't real ghosts we see, but mere memories from people who used to be here." I ran with that. "So it wasn't Mom that we saw, it was the memory of her because she used to go to school here."

Dad thought about my words for a moment. When he nodded, I couldn't tell if he believed me or if he was just grasping onto something in order to keep his sanity. "That's why she didn't talk to us," he said. "It wasn't really her."

I nodded, trying to convince myself that he was right.

"What do you think that meant?" I asked him. "Up and around, tickle the troll, find your way down, and pay the toll?"

Dad shook his head and pushed up to his feet. He gave a little chuckle and said, "That's just like your mom to keep us guessing, isn't it?"

The wistfulness to his tone echoed the way I felt. "I think so. Was she always like that?"

Dad nodded as he led the way to the stairs. I scooted around the direct moonlight from the window so I wouldn't show up in the corridor in wolf form. I was sure Don Ruvine would appreciate that.

"Your mother was always a mystery to me," Dad admitted as I followed him down the steps. "She was like sunshine. You couldn't keep her bottled up and no matter where she went, she made everything seem that much brighter. Yet, because of her past and her werewolf heritage, she held a side I couldn't follow or relate to. She kept it deep within her, but I felt it there in times when she was quiet. I'd ask, 'Silvia, are you alright?' and she would smile at me and say with her sunshine returning, 'Of course, Stephen. I'm with you.'" He paused on the fourth floor and gave me a small smile. "You'll learn someday that werewolves love with all of their heart. It's a rare thing in this world, and a gift. I was honored to hold such a precious gift in my hands."

He continued down, but I waited on the steps to collect myself. I had seldom asked about my mother because I knew how hard it was for Dad to talk about her. To hear such things like 'she was like sunshine' and 'she held a side I couldn't follow' made her feel more real than ever. I blinked quickly at the thought of the ghost we had followed above and how badly he had wanted to talk to her.

My mother got sick and passed away when I was four and Drake was three. My dad eventually married Julianne who was wonderful and loving and took great care of us, but there was something to be said about living a life and raising children with the woman he had loved since they met right out of high school. He would always love her, and her loss had taken more from him than I even imagined.

"What took you so long?" I heard Drake ask from the bottom of the stairs. "The Headmistress addressed the parents and a lot have already gone home."

"What did she say?" Dad asked with forced lightness in his tone.

"That there's some sort of demon danger here along with the ghosts and that they have a team dedicated to keeping the students safe, something like that," Drake replied. "I wish I could see a demon."

A smile touched my face. My fifteen-year-old brother never thought to censor what he said. I had no doubt students and other parents were staring at him because of his words.

I ran down the rest of the stairs and met them at the bottom. Sure enough, I caught several looks of disapproval before individuals turned away.

"I've got a lot of homework," I told Dad. "It's probably time for you to head home."

"That's it?" Drake replied. "But I wanted to meet a dragon and have a magician show me a trick."

"There aren't magicians here," I replied. "They're called witches and warlocks, and they don't just do tricks on command."

"I could do one."

I turned at Brack's deep voice. The huge warlock grinned down at me.

"Did you parents leave?" I asked.

He nodded. "They, uh, had to hurry."

"I'm sorry I didn't get to meet them."

He gave a massive shrug and said, "They're afraid of werewolves."

I couldn't imagine anyone Brack's size being afraid of a werewolf, but it wasn't my place to argue. I caught a questioning look on Dad's face and figured it would be easier not to get into it.

"You want to show Drake what you can do?" I asked Brack.

He nodded. "Watch." He pointed at the front door.

Mrs. Hassleton was busy saying farewell to Martus' parents. The boy was in my Care of Green Multicellular Organisms class, called such because Professor Seedly hated the term 'plant'. Martus was a taniwha whose family only ate bugs. He and his parents had slimy-looking skin because they usually lived in the water.

"Take care, Mr. and Mrs. Phagen," Mrs. Hassleton was saying. "See yourselves safely home."

She pulled on the door, but it didn't open. Mrs. Hassleton gave them an apologetic smile and tried again, but it still didn't budge.

"Are you doing that?" Drake asked.

Brack nodded but kept his focus on the door. "She doesn't like Finn."

I was touched and embarrassed that he was using his affinity out of some sort of protectiveness over me.

"It's alright, Brack. Let her open it now," I told him.

Brack closed his eyes and Mrs. Hassleton opened the door.

"Geesh, strange door," she said by way of apology to the Phagens. "It doesn't normally act up."

"Have a good night," Mr. Phagen told her before he led his wife through the massive door.

Mrs. Hassleton shut it behind them, then opened it again as if afraid it would stick. When it opened, she gave the door a relieved look and left it partially ajar.

"That was awesome!" Drake said.

Brack beamed at the compliment.

"That's some trick," Dad told the hulking student. "I would definitely be playing tricks on my students if I could do that."

"You have students?" Brack asked in surprise.

Dad nodded. "I teach high school science. Maybe if I could lock my students in the classroom, they would actually learn something."

Brack gave a laugh so loud it echoed around the room.

Dad and Drake both stared at him. I took the opportunity to escort them to the door.

"Well, uh, thanks for visiting," I said. "I'll let you know when the next parent night is. And please tell Juli thanks for the stroganoff."

I looked around quickly and found the bag sitting at the bottom of the stairs where I had dropped it when I ran after Dad.

"I'll tell her," Dad said. He still looked a bit stunned from all that he had seen.

"Make sure he gets home," I told Drake quietly.

My brother nodded. "I will. I hope I'm a werewolf so I can come here," he said.

"Me, too," I replied levelly. Inwardly I cringed at all I had come up against as a werewolf in a school that was still recovering from the damage my uncle had left behind. "Take care and text me."

"I will," Drake promised. "You too."

I nodded and followed them through the door. The sight of the buildings of New York reaching around us surprised me. It was easy to forget that we were in the middle of such a huge city. The Academy felt apart from anything around us, as if we were in our own world.

"I want to show you something," I said before they could go down the steps. "You wanted to see a dragon, Drake? Look."

I pulled back the sleeve of my shirt to reveal Sparrow sleeping around my wrist. She had begun to stir during my trips up and down the stairs. It was time for her to eat, anyway, so I didn't see the harm of letting them watch her hunt.

"Is that real?" Drake asked, staring.

Sparrow's head lifted and she looked at him. Her red forked tongue flicked out as she tasted the air.

41

"Whoa!" Drake exclaimed.

"That's really a dragon?" my dad said in awe.

I nodded. "Are you hungry, Sparrow?" I asked her.

The black and purple dragon unwound herself and crossed to my palm. Her green eyes blinked and she shook herself, unfurling her black wings.

Moths fluttered around the Academy lights on either side of the towering doors. I lifted her up so she could see them.

"It's been a while since she's eaten," I told my dad and brother. "You can watch her."

Sparrow's gaze locked on one of the moths. I could feel her little claws prick my skin as she readied herself. She lifted her wings, gave one flap, and darted toward the insects.

Within a few seconds, the little dragon was sitting on my shoulder finishing her mothy meal.

"That was incredible!" Drake exclaimed.

"Yes," Dad said. "Your mother mentioned little dragons, but I never thought I would actually see one."

I ran a finger down her back. "She's a sylph dragon. They're actually very rare. I'm supposed to keep her hidden." I couldn't help smiling when I said, "She chose me after she hatched, so I'm her keeper."

"That's so cool," Drake said. "I hope I have a dragon when I come here."

Dad and I exchanged a look. I know we both hoped Drake would never have a reason to attend Haunted High. As amazing as the Academy was, life had been so much simpler before the accident in which Sebastian had died and I found myself in the form of a wolf for the first time in my life. I didn't wish that on Drake or anyone else.

Sparrow finished eating and climbed back down to my hand.

"Is she going to sleep again?" Drake asked.

I nodded. "Professor Seedly she'll eventually spend more and more time awake, but since she's only a few days old, she sleeps most of the time."

"Just like any other baby," Dad said with a satisfied nod.

They watched as she wrapped snuggly around my wrist, oblivious to any danger. I slid my sleeve back down.

"Get home safe and give Juli my love," I said.

"We will," Dad promised.

I walked back into the Academy feeling heavier and lighter at the same time.

Mrs. Hassleton had found something near her office to occupy her time so she didn't have to say goodbye to my family. I shot her a look when I walked by, but she pretended not to notice.

"Are you sure Amryn didn't run away due to the presence of a werewolf tainting the Academy?" Don Ruvine asked loudly when I walked by the coven leader and Vicken on my way to the stairs.

"I told you Finn has been trying to help find her," Vicken replied. "But I can't say he's been quick about it."

I bent and picked up the bag, straightening in time to see Don Ruvine shake his head. "Don't trust a werewolf, son. You'll only regret it."

I met Vicken's gaze across the room. He looked away the moment our eyes met and led his dad to the door.

"I'll find Amryn. You worry about Mother. Let me know as soon as she's safe," Vicken told his father.

"I will," Don Ruvine replied. "Keep yourself safe."

"I will," Vicken said.

Relief filled me when the vampire left the Academy. I hadn't realized how tight my muscles had been. When they relaxed, I felt my instincts whisper about the danger I had been in. Vicken gave me a questioning look. I turned away and carried the bag up the stairs. The smell of stroganoff kept me climbing until I reached the thirteenth floor. I walked to the window and sat beneath it where my father and I had been. When I cracked the Tupperware container, the welcoming smell of Julianne's homemade pasta chased away any other thought.

I stayed there longer than I should have. Deep down, I knew that I hoped my mother would appear again. It had felt like something out of a dream to see her standing where I sat. Her smile was burned in my mind. I would never forget it.

"Up and around, tickle the troll, find your way down, and pay the toll," I repeated. I wondered what it meant.

I ran a finger down Sparrow's sleeping form and said it again. "Up and around, tickle the troll, find your way down, and pay the toll."

My ears caught the sound of footsteps in the secret passageway just past the end of the stairs. I wasn't surprised when I heard the latch catch. The door swung inward and Professor Briggs stepped out.

"At a meeting?" I asked.

He nodded as he closed the door carefully behind him. "We can't be too careful. With the ghosts not responding to the Grims, we need to find other options. We can't have ghosts causing disturbances in our classrooms."

"They seem harmless for the most part," I replied.

Professor Briggs took several limping steps toward me. He put his weight heavily on his cane, reminding me that he had just climbed several flights on his leg that had been heavily damaged by demon fire the night my uncle attacked the Academy.

His dark robes hid most of the scars from the attack, but those on his hand and the jagged scar down his left cheek were harder to hide. He leaned against the wall and gave me an appraising look.

"Did you have a good visit with your family?"

I nodded. "My dad and brother came. My stepmother is seven months pregnant and not feeling good, so she stayed home." I lifted the container of stroganoff I had only been able to finish half of. "But she sent one of her best meals. Want to try it?"

Despite my thought that he would turn me down, Professor Briggs actually looked tempted. "It's been longer than I can remember since I've had a homecooked meal." He gave a smile that was twisted by his scar. "Don't get me wrong. Mr. Handsworth crafts some amazing food for the cafeteria, but it's not the same. Group meals and all that."

"Try it," I said, offering it up.

Professor Briggs crossed to me and, after hesitating only the slightest, slid to a painful seat across from me. He set the cane down and accept the container I held out.

"You'll have to ignore my germs," I said, indicating the plastic fork on top. "It's all we've got."

"I'm sure I'll survive," Professor Briggs said wryly. He pried the top off the Tupperware and breathed deeply of the pasta scent. "If this is half as good as it smells...," he began.

"You can finish it," I told him with a smile. "I've had my fill and I'm worried that if I try to keep it in the cafeteria refrigerator, the warlocks will find it."

Professor Briggs nodded. "We warlocks do have a thing for food."

He took a bite of the pasta. A smile of bliss spread across his face and he leaned back against the wall to savor the bite.

"This is probably the best thing I've ever had in my life," he declared.

It made me happy to see him so relaxed. Briggs was always busy teaching or training or preparing to teach or train. I couldn't recall seeing him ever take a break except for reading from his heavy tomes at the back of his candlelit classroom.

The thought occurred to me to ask, "Professor Briggs, why is it that the rest of the classrooms are lit by electricity and yours is the only one lit by candles? It's kind-of eerie."

He gave me an assessing look. "I could tell you what I tell the rest of the students, or I can tell you the real truth."

"I want the real truth," I replied, intrigued. "But what do you tell the rest of the students?"

He chuckled and admitted, "I tell them I'm afraid of electricity."

I snorted at the thought of the professor being afraid of anything and said, "Do they really believe that?"

He twirled another forkful around the tines and said with a half-smile, "They don't dare to call me a liar."

I laughed and sat back. "Do you like that your students are afraid of you?"

He took a bite and chewed, then swallowed before he said, "Are you afraid of me?"

"I was my first day here," I admitted. "When I found out I had two classes with you, I was about to quit right then."

Briggs chuckled again and said, "I tried to intimidate you in the hopes that you would leave."

"I know, and it almost worked." I realized he had distracted me from my question and asked, "So what's the truth? Why do you have candles? That must be a pain to keep changing."

Professor Briggs took another bite and waited until he was done before he said, "I had a friend with an affinity for electricity."

"Another warlock?" I asked, surprised.

He nodded. "We were in school together. He would always mess with the lights. The professors hated it. But one time he showed me how he could pull electricity from an outlet or a light source and play with it. He held it in his hand like your dragon and let it dance above his palms. It was fascinating." Briggs shook his head with an expression of wonder.

His gaze darkened and he said, "Then a rat came into the room from a crack in the wall. Stith pointed his finger at it and the electricity shot from his hand and electrocuted the rat." Briggs shook his head. "Stith actually laughed when the poor creature lay there twitching. He only pretended to feel bad when the telepath the rat belonged to came looking for it and found it dead."

He had been twirling pasta on the fork as if he didn't realize he was doing it. He paused and looked at me and said, "Stith told me he had killed larger creatures. There was no remorse on his face, only excitement as if he wanted to do it again. After the things he showed me, I stopped trusting electricity and asked Headmaster Wrengold to change the Academy over to candles, but the Headmaster refused, saying it was too costly and a fire hazard. I insisted on lighting my own room that way when I became a professor."

"Where did Stith go?" I asked, horrified and intrigued at the same time.

"I lost track of him after he graduated. He wasn't thrilled with the fact that I was given a professor position." Briggs winked at me. "We were pretty unruly children, so I couldn't blame him." He straightened his back and winced as if it hurt to sit on the floor. He continued with, "But after so many professors and students had been killed by your uncle, we knew if we didn't do something, the Academy would shut down. Those of us who had been professors' aides during our senior year asked to be allowed to teach. We grew up quickly after that."

There was a wistfulness on his face that made me wonder if he regretted letting go of his childhood to take over teaching. I had never thought about how hard it must have been to teach his peers. No wonder he kept up such a haughty appearance. None of the students who acted out in my other classes dared to do so in Briggs'.

He finished the stroganoff in silence.

Chapter Four

AS PROFESSOR BRIGGS SCRAPED the last of the stroganoff from the container, I whispered to myself, "Up and around, tickle the troll, find your way down, and pay the toll." I had the cadence in my head and couldn't keep from repeating it in my mind.

Professor Briggs paused with his last forkful halfway to his mouth and looked at me. "Where did you hear that?"

I knew the truth would make me sound crazy, but I told him, "Dad and I followed my mother's ghost up here. She said it before she disappeared out the window."

Briggs dropped the fork. It landed in the Tupperware with a dull thud.

"Silvia Roe's ghost was here?" he said in shock.

I nodded.

He gestured with the container as if he forgot that he held it. The fork rattled back and forth when he said, "And she told you that?"

I nodded again. "She repeated it twice before she left. She wouldn't talk to me or my dad. All she said was, 'Up and around, tickle the troll, find your way down, and pay the toll.' Do you know what it means?" The thought that the professor might actually understand my mother's cryptic words gave me hope.

"I know what it means," Briggs said. His face was white as if he had been the one to see the ghost. His voice dropped to a whisper and he said, "I had almost forgotten."

"Forgotten what?" I asked.

"She's the ghost of your heart!" Briggs exclaimed. "Just like the first ghost told you. She gave you a clue!"

"But I don't know what it means," I replied, rising. The thought that she was the ghost of my heart instead of Sebastian made sense, but her words did not. "How are we supposed to figure it out?" I held out a hand to help the professor up.

"Get your team together," Briggs told me. He waved my hand away and struggled to his feet. "We've got work to do."

"Now?" I asked. I glanced out the window. "It's the middle of the night."

"Now," he replied. "Hurry."

I returned with my exhausted team in tow. Vicken had grumbled the whole way up about climbing thirteen flights of stairs just to appease a demanding werewolf. The other two vampires from our team follow him without a word. I had found Alden and Dara asleep in their rooms, but it had taken some time to track down Lyris and Brack. I finally found the witch and the warlock in the library practicing from the leather-bound book they had received on their first day of training. Apparently, they had also seen the green flames in the eyes of the ghost during parent night.

A few ghosts followed Alden up the stairs.

"Uh, what's with your new friends?" Dara asked.

Alden glanced behind him. "They've started following me since my parents left. I think they're hoping I can get them to the beyond, but I don't know how." He shook his head. "I told them that, but they don't listen."

"It's a bit creepy," Lyris said.

"Yeah, it's worse at night for sure," Alden agreed.

"It's not like you could wait until some normal hour of the day, weremutt," Vicken continued speaking from the back of the group. "Some of us who aren't flea-bitten mutts actually enjoy sleep."

"Give Finn-wolf a break," Lyris said.

"I'll give you a break," Vicken threatened.

"I'll break your back," Brack replied.

Dara gave an exasperated sigh and said, "Shut up, everyone!"

I reached the top step and crossed to Professor Briggs without a word. At least having the five of them between Vicken and I had made it easier to ignore my instincts and stay in human form. If it was just the two of us, I couldn't say that I had the control to ignore him after all his father had said to mine combined with the demands of the moonlight through the windows.

Professor Briggs didn't seem to hear us despite Vicken's complaining. He was staring out the window, his gaze distant as though he saw something beyond the rooftop and the building walls that surrounded Haunted High. When I set a hand on his shoulder, he startled and turned.

"We're here, Professor. What do you need us to do?" I asked.

He appeared taken aback for a moment.

"The rhyme from my mom, remember?" I reminded him.

He nodded. "Oh, right. The rhyme." He cleared his throat and straightened with his cane for support. He met the gazes of the tired team members behind me. "You don't know the particulars of what we're talking about, but I need you to trust me. Brack, open the window."

Everyone pressed to the walls on either side to let the huge warlock through. Brack struggled against the tightly shut window and let out a breath when it finally budged and slid up.

"Now everyone, onto the roof."

"What?" Lyris asked in surprise.

"He's trying to kill us all," Dara replied dryly.

I had already been on the roof once. That was enough to know how steep the sides were and how easy it was to slide to the edge.

"Are you sure about this?" I asked him as I crawled carefully out.

He nodded. "As sure as your mother's words."

I placed my feet carefully on the moonlit roof and stepped gingerly toward the middle to make room for the others. A shiver ran down my spine at the feeling of the moonlight on my shoulders. The last time I had been on the roof was in wolf form. It was far harder to keep my footing with four paws than two feet. I gritted my teeth and concentrated on maintaining my human form.

"What does that mean?" Vicken asked grumpily from the back of the group as he finally climbed through the window.

"Need to know basis," Briggs told him.

"I'm following your orders onto a roof," Vicken replied. "I think I need to know."

"Time will tell," Briggs said evasively as he climbed out to join us.

The professor waved for me to continue. I could hear his limping steps and realized it must be far harder for him than any of us to keep his footing with his limp. Everyone walked with their arms out, balancing carefully with a foot on either side of the peak of the roof. By the time we reached the end, I heard my teammates sigh in relief, but I was the one left staring down at the ground far below.

"Uh, now what, Professor?" I asked over my shoulder.

"Say the chant," Briggs called back.

I shook my head, sure he was losing it. "Up and around, tickle the troll, find your way down, then pay the toll."

"What garbage is that?" Vicken muttered.

"So do it," Briggs said, ignoring the vampire.

"Do what?" I asked, glancing back at him. "There's nowhere else to go."

"Feel with your feet," he told me. "Go up and around."

Dara waited right behind me. She gave me a look that said she thought the professor was crazy.

"We need to go back inside," Lyris said. "I don't like heights."

"Ha!" Vicken exclaimed from his place in front of the professor. "A witch who's afraid of heights? That's hilarious!"

"Like a vampire who's afraid of fire?" Lyris shot back with a tremble in her voice.

"I'll make you pay for that," Vicken said.

He pushed forward in his attempt to reach her. Jean, the blue-haired vampire in front of him, stumbled, shoving Lorne and then Lyris. Dara bumped into me. My heart leaped in my chest as I fell forward into the empty air that was all that separated me from the ground far below.

"Finn!" Dara called out.

Instead of plummeting to the ground, I landed on some sort of invisible platform. My heart thundered in my ears as I looked around, confirming that I wasn't about to die. I slid my hands over the surface. It felt rough like wood. I followed the steps to invisible walls that ran upward. I followed them and found that they went higher than my head.

"It's an invisible staircase," I said in shock.

"Up and around," Briggs repeated from the back of the group without the amazement that showed on the faces of my teammates.

I pushed to my feet and took another tentative step upward. I could see the alley far below. There appeared to be nothing between me and falling to my death. The effect was unsettling. Nevertheless, the urgency in the professor's voice beckoned me forward. I took a step, then another. The stairs wound around and upward in a tight spiral so that I could see my teammates climbing slowly beneath me. I held onto an invisible railing with the fear that I might step and find that a stair was broken or missing. Fortunately, I reached the top without incident and found the shape of a door beneath my fingertips.

"Okay, professor. Now what?" I called down.

Before he could tell me to, I repeated my mother's saying, "Up and around, tickle the troll, find your way down, and pay the toll. So, tickle the troll. What does that mean?" I asked aloud.

"It's a word game," Dara replied from behind me. "What's in front of you?"

"A door," I said. I ran my fingers along it. "There's a shape carved here."

"Could it be a troll?" she asked.

I followed the edges from the top to the bottom. The outline was carved deep and looped around. "If the troll's arms are up and his feet nearly as thick as his torso, then yeah," I replied.

"His arms are up," Dara repeated. "Tickle his armpits."

I shook my head, but did as she instructed. The moment my fingers touched both of his armpits at the same time, the door swung open to reveal a small platform with a slide leading down.

"Let me guess," Dara said wryly over my shoulder. "Find your way down?"

"Looks like it," I replied.

Lyris came up behind us. "Vicken's going to be mad to go down when we just climbed up." The tremor in her voice told of how hard it had been for her to take the invisible staircase.

"Oh, a slide!" Alden said from behind her. "I love slides!"

"He would," Dara grumbled in my ear.

I stifled a smile and sat down on the edge of the dark tube. Before I was ready, Dara shoved me from behind. I slid through the darkness about half as far as we had climbed and then flew out onto a pile of cushions. I heard someone else in the slide and rolled to the side before Dara could land on me. I grabbed her hand and pulled her out of the way just before Lyris plummeted onto the cushions.

"Thanks," Dara said.

We helped Lyris and Alden. The tube rumbled with deep laughter before Brack flew out and hit the cushions with a resounding thud. We all tried to pull him up, but Lorne and then Jean landed on the laughing warlock before he would move.

Vicken tumbled out of the slide and fell on his stomach with a muffled oomph.

"You might want to move," I suggested when nobody stepped forward to help the vampire.

"Why?" Vicken snarled.

"You're about to be a pancake," Lyris pointed out.

At the sound of Professor Briggs sliding toward the exit, Vicken scrambled ungracefully to his feet and moved out of the way. To our surprise, the professor slid to a stop just before flying out. He put his cane on the ground and hopped down as if he did it every day.

At our stares, Professor Briggs allowed himself a small smile before he said, "Control is key."

He limped past us toward a short door at the end. There was no handle; instead a cup with the words 'Toll please' written in gold had been fastened to the middle.

"What's the toll?" I asked.

"Will someone tell me what you're talking about?" Vicken replied. "You sound like an idiot."

"At least he doesn't look like an idiot," I heard Alden replied under his breath.

I glanced back to see that Vicken's long black hair he always kept pulled back in a ponytail had come free on his landing and was an unruly mess that stuck out everywhere. I met Alden's eyes and smothered a laugh. The Grim grinned back at me.

"Silvia was particular about her tolls," Briggs said. He fumbled inside the sleeves of his robe for a moment. "Ah. This will do!"

He pulled out a marble and set it in the cup. The was a slight puffing sound as though the marble had been sucked into a vacuum and the door opened inward. When I glanced in the cup as I passed, I found that it was empty. I ducked through the door and then rose to find myself standing in the middle of a small room.

"Where are we?" Lyris asked in amazement.

The rest of the team squeezed in. It took both Jean and Lorne to push Brack through, but finally we all stood inside. The room looked like the inside of a treehouse. Wood covered the ground, floors, and ceiling. Sentences had been written along the panels in bright paint in a language I didn't know. I recognized my mother's handwriting from the shopping list my dad still kept on our refrigerator and ran my fingers along it.

"This is a clubhouse," I said.

I realized it was true as I took in the piles of items in one corner that students might horde, like old books, crates, and cups filled with pencils, pens, scissors, and even a few utensils. Drawings of dragons, a few of demons, and one picture sketched in purple of a hulking beast in the middle of flames occupied the far wall. Several wooden chairs and a small table took up a corner. Professor Briggs made his way to one of the chairs and sat down. The sheen of sweat on his forehead told of the toll the journey had taken on his battered body, but he didn't complain.

"Yes, this is a clubhouse," the professor said, his voice tight. "It was our clubhouse."

"Who all came here?" Alden asked in amazement as he looked around.

The lines that surrounded the professor's eyes deepened when he said, "Me, Zanie, Parken, Stith, Silvia, and Branch. This was our escape from the Academy."

"What did you do here?" Dara asked.

"It doesn't matter," Vicken said, cutting her off. He glared around the small room. "Why are we here? This is ridiculous. We're wasting time when we could be finding Amryn."

Professor Briggs spoke with the calm voice required of a teacher of monsters. "Amryn was taken by demons. According to the ghost who attacked Finn, we need to find the key to the door that his uncle unlocked. If we can find the door, we can hopefully find your sister, but if we're unable to lock it when we find it, we may let out the rest of the demons and doom the Academy entirely, not to mention the rest of the world."

"So we're looking for a clue to where the key might be?" Alden supplied helpfully.

Professor Briggs nodded. "Look everywhere. The ghost of Finn's mom must have led him here for a reason."

We searched the entire room. Fortunately, there weren't many places to look. Unfortunately, there was nothing to find. By the time we gave up, Vicken was in an even worse mood.

"You're all lunatics," he said. "You believe the words of Finn's mom's ghost even though the Grims said they're merely reliving memories? This is ridiculous."

I clenched my hands into fists, letting the pain of my palm keep me centered before I could retaliate.

"I'm afraid Vicken may be right."

I turned at the sound of defeat in Professor Briggs' voice. He gave me an apologetic look. "I had hoped she was trying to tell you something, but I think we may all have been following just a memory."

I shook my head. "It was too real."

"Oh, poor Finn," Vicken replied in a singsong voice. "Did your mommy tell you wrong?"

His words destroyed the last of my self-control. I lunged at him and was caught with my hands inches from his throat. Brack, Lyris, Alden, and Dara pulled me back before I could strangle the vampire.

Vicken laughed, but I could tell by the tightness of his voice that he had actually been afraid for a moment. "Calm down, little weremutt. You can leave the Academy as soon as you find my sister and go crying home to your pathetic human daddy. It'll all be fine."

"You're taking out your worry for your mother and sister on Finn," Dara said.

Vicken glared at her and his hands clenched into fists, but instead of attacking, he turned around and faced the slide. "How do I get out of this blasted place?"

I pushed their hands away and stood. "I'm alright," I said. My fingers itched to attack again, but I ignored the impulse. "You can let me go." I looked at the professor. "Maybe you're right. We should all leave."

Professor Briggs nodded. "Vicken, sit on the edge of the slide and say 'up'." He smiled at Lyris' amazed look. "Branch was very good with physics spells."

"That's amazing!" Lyris said when Vicken did as the professor asked and slid in reverse up the slide.

Everyone else took their turn until Professor Briggs and I were the last in the clubhouse.

"I'm sorry we didn't find anything," Briggs said. "I really hoped we would."

"Me, too," I admitted. "I guess we just need more time to figure out what the ghost meant. It's neat to find a place where my mom was, though."

He nodded. "She really liked it in here. We all did." He gestured toward the slide. "You first."

I shook my head. "I think I'll stay here for a bit."

He nodded with an understanding expression. "Try to get some sleep tonight. You still have class in the morning."

"Don't remind me," I replied with a groan.

He chuckled and sat on the edge of the slide with his damaged leg held carefully out in front of him. He set the cane on his lap and said "Up," in a commanding tone.

The professor slid up the tube and out of sight. I took a seat on one of the chairs and studied the writing on the wall. Briggs had said the words were sayings, poems, or anything else the students found inspiring writing in a variety of mythic languages. Lyris and Dara had translated all the words, but didn't find anything helpful. Though they weren't the key, I found myself drawn to my mother's handwriting. I wished I could read the language and vowed to study harder in Professor Mellon's class.

Sparrow stirred from around my wrist. She climbed onto my palm and made a little mewling noise.

"Hey girl," I said to her. "Good to see you awake." I lifted my hand so she could see the clubhouse. "Want to explore?"

I smiled when she took the words to heart. The tiny dragon flew from my hand and darted around the little room. She climbed up the wooden walls and even licked one of the words as if checking to see if the paint tasted good. It apparently didn't because she took off again, exploring the boxes, the cups of writing implements, and beneath the table. At first I hoped she might lead me to a clue, but then it became clear she was just filled with enthusiasm like a puppy brought outside for the first time.

I marveled at the fact that there was no dust in the clubhouse. I wondered if one of Briggs and my mother's friends had an affinity for controlling dust. It may not have been the most exciting warlock skill, but it would definitely have its uses. All in all, it amazed me to be sitting there in a clubhouse where my mother used to escape with her friends. The path there and the presence of the clubhouse itself was incredible, and I felt closer to her just by being there.

Eventually, Sparrow grew tired and curled up to sleep around my wrist again. I ran my finger down her spikes the way she seemed to like and soon her breathing steadied into a whispery cadence I could barely hear. A sound on the slide made me wonder how long I had been there.

Dara appeared and didn't seem the least bit surprised at finding me still there. I suspected Professor Briggs had sent her to check on me.

"Hey," she said when she stood and attempted to straighten her long ash-colored hair after her unceremonious landing on the cushions.

"Hey," I replied, unsure what else to say.

Dara took a seat next to me and looked around the room. "This is pretty neat," she admitted.

I nodded. "It would be a good place to go when you feel overwhelmed with everyone's emotions."

She gave me a sideways look, her violet eyes guarded. "I thought, well, with it being your mom's clubhouse and everything...."

I smiled at her. "Dara, you're more than welcome to come here. She would have liked that."

The empath gave a little sound of consideration and turned away so I couldn't see her face. She picked a pen from one of the cups and turned it over in her hand.

"I don't know what it's like, really," she said quietly.

"What what's like?" I probed.

She was silent a moment before she said, "What it's like to have a parent who cares about you enough to lead you to this place."

That caught me off-guard. I hadn't thought of my mother's appearance like that. It was hard not to think of it as just another of the Grim's so-called memory ghosts living out snippets of their life without any realization that we could see them. The thought of Mom giving me the secret to her special place at the Academy made me feel warm inside, as though I wasn't so alone.

I started to smile, then realized Dara wasn't smiling at all. In fact, even with her head turned, I could see tears running down her cheek. I heard a quiet catch in her breath that she tried to hide. It took me a moment to remember that her parents hadn't been at parent night. She had refused to let the Headmistress invite them at all. From what she had told me, her parents had abused her empath skills and used her to take away the pains they didn't care to avoid because she was there. Her whole life had been spent carrying the pain of others, and those who should have valued her the most had abused her.

I put my hand on her back. "This clubhouse can be both of ours," I told her. "Come here whenever you want. I won't tell anyone."

She sniffed and looked at me with watery eyes. "Really?"

"Definitely," I replied, giving her my warmest smile. "Everyone needs an escape once in a while."

She shook her head. "How are you so strong all the time?"

I stared at her. "I'm not strong at all," I admitted, lowering my gaze. "To tell you the truth, I'm barely holding on here. It was nice to see my dad and brother, but even the possibility of Drake turning into a werewolf terrifies me." My voice dropped and I said, "I thought it would be easier than this."

Chapter Five

WE BOTH FELL QUIET. Only the sound of Sparrow's tiny breaths and Dara's heartbeat met my ears. I hadn't realized my hand was still on Dara's back until I felt the lessening of pain in my right hand. It always throbbed. Dr. Six had mentioned that it might hurt forever. As much as my palm ached, I couldn't imagine being covered in the types of wounds Professor Briggs had from the same fire. It made me respect the warlock even more.

I didn't realize how much my hand hurt until the ache disappeared. I heard Dara's intake of breath and my heart skipped a beat at the thought that she was taking my pain. I jerked my hands back and tipped over on the flimsy wooden chair. I landed on the floor with a hard thump. Sparrow stirred, but didn't awaken.

"Finn, I—" Dara began.

"Dara, you don't deserve my pain," I said from the floor.

"But you could use a break," she replied. "I can give you that." Her eyebrows formed a little furrow between them when she looked down at me and said, "The pain is intense."

I couldn't downplay it because she would know the lie. Instead, I glanced around, searching for something light to say. My eyes fell on a mark scratched into the bottom of the table. The familiarity of it pushed at the back of my mind. I had seen it somewhere, of that I was sure.

"It's a sign," I said, staring.

"Being in pain isn't a sign," Dara replied. "And you don't have to suffer needlessly. That's why I—"

I shook my head. "No. It's a sign! Look!"

I scrambled to my feet and pushed the table over. She stared at me as if I had gone made. But when I pointed at the mark, her eyes widened.

"It's a sigil," Dara breathed.

"It's not a bird," I replied, studying the mark that look nothing like the ocean fowl she mentioned. The symbol was a square with a half circle inside and three lines through it.

A small laugh escaped her and she said, "Not a seagull, a sigil. It's a symbol of a specific demon. The mark itself is the demon's signature." She let out a breath and shook her head. "This is a powerful demon."

"Could it be Chutka?" I asked.

She turned her violet eyes on me. "Where did you hear that name?"

"The professors keep mentioning it, and the demon that burned my hand said it before he died. So did the ghost my brother talked to. I have a feeling this is all connected."

Dara's face paled. She backed away from the table. "Chutka the Shambler is no ordinary demon. If he's at the bottom of this, we're in a lot of trouble."

I nodded. "That's why the Headmistress and the professors are so scared. Maybe they think this Chutka will come through the door." I reached out a hand to touch the sigil.

"Finn, don't," Dara whispered.

I glanced back at her and was amazed at the fear on her face. She hadn't looked that frightened even when the demon attacked in the corridor. I pulled my hand back.

"I've seen this symbol before," I told her, rising.

"Where?"

"I can't remember," I admitted. "I keep going over the image in my mind. It's written on a box, but I can't figure out where it would be."

"Show me," she said.

Caught off-guard, I replied, "What?"

"Show me," she said, holding out her hand. "It's a werewolf thing, right? You can show me the memory and maybe I can figure out where it is."

I shook my head. "I don't think that's a good idea."

"Why not?" she asked.

I glanced at the sigil, then back at her. "The first and last time I tried to show someone something, it went wrong."

I winced inward at the memory. I had tried to show Lorne the memories a fox in Creature Languages had given to me. It was more of a moment of pride than anything else, and the memory turned, giving me no control until I showed him the accident in which Sebastian had died and I had become a werewolf. It had left us both shaken.

"You can trust me," Dara said, her voice encouraging and filled with understanding. "It might be our only chance to stop whatever demon is linked to this sigil."

I knew she was right. We didn't have any other leads.

The sound of a bell caught my ear. The thought of sitting through class wasn't a welcome one. I held out a hand. "It's worth a try."

Dara motioned to the chairs and we both took a seat. She set her hand in mine and closed her eyes. I studied her face. As an empath, Dara was one of the most closed-off people I had ever met. Usually her gaze was either accusing or angry. I couldn't blame her after all she had been through, but it was nice to be able to look at her without fearing her wrath.

She was beautiful with her features relaxed and with trust on her face. It caught me by surprise to realize it and I must have stared at her longer than I planned because she opened one eye and gave me a skeptical look.

"Are we doing this?" she asked with an edge to her voice.

I nodded quickly and closed my eyes. "Just keep your mind open," I said. "I'll do the rest."

"How do I know if my mind's open?" she asked.

I opened my eyes and smiled at her concerned expression. "I have no idea. We'll just give it a try."

"Alright," she replied. She closed her eyes again.

I shut my eyes and let out a slow breath, but my mind raced with thoughts of the sigil, the feeling of Dara's hand in mine, and the thought that we were both missing breakfast. My stomach growled, reminding me that werewolves are fond of food. I counted to ten, willing my mind to clear. It was something Julianne had taught me to do whenever I got frustrated. It worked to calm my whirlwind of thoughts and let me concentrate.

I found the memory I wanted and pushed it at Dara. I pictured the memory traveling down my arm and through my fingertips to where they rested in Dara's hand. My fingers tingled as the memory passed from me to her. I felt Dara's hand twitch in her surprise, then her movements stilled as the memory flowed over us both.

The square with the half circle inside of it and three lines through it grew clear in my mind. It had indeed been written on a box in black marker. The box was cardboard and looked ordinary except for the sigil drawn on it. As I watched, the memory pulled back, allowing me to see more. My heart slowed as I recognized our attic at home. My father was there moving boxes to the far corner to make room for our Christmas decorations we had just put away.

"I've never had the heart to get rid of these," he was saying to Julianne. "I guess it's silly."

She shook her head. "The boys will be happy to have some of Silvia's things when they get older. You should keep them."

Julianne smiled at me as I played in Dad's old box of G.I. Joes. He brought it out once in a while if Drake and I promised to keep track of the pieces and to be careful when we put the weapons in the soldiers' hands so the fingers didn't stretch out or break.

"Who's ready for dinner?" she asked.

I jumped up. "I am!"

"Last one to the table's a rotten banana," Drake called behind me.

We raced down the ladder from the attic and ran toward the kitchen.

The memory faded and then changed before I could take my hand from Dara's. My fingers tightened when I saw the white room. The beeping sound that used to bother me was slower than usual. Then the beeping stopped entirely. The doctor used some sort of humming device. My mother's body lurched and then settled on the bed again. Tears were streaming down my father's face from the other side of the room. I held Drake's hand as we both stood forgotten in the corner. The doctor met my father's gaze and shook his head. Dad covered his face with his hands and sobbed.

The memory faded and I dropped Dara's hand. I put my bandaged one over my face before she could see the tears on my cheeks.

"Finn, I can help," she began.

I shook my head without looking at her. "I can handle it," I said. I hated that my voice cracked, betraying me. I had relieved the memory of my mother's death more times than I could count, but it was harder after seeing her in the hallway and hearing her voice for the first time in twelve years.

When I was four, I hadn't understood what happened when she died. All I remembered was visiting her in the hospital after she got sick. It wasn't until later that I found out she had been battling cancer and then contracted pneumonia. She had only lasted a few weeks after that. On the day we visited, Dad said she might be able to go home, but she took a hard turn for the worse.

They should have had us leave when she started coughing, but everyone forgot about the two children in the corner in their rush to save our mother. I had asked Drake about it once, but he didn't remember. The thought had given me some comfort even though I had woken up screaming for Mom for nearly six months afterwards.

Dara set a hand on my arm. I wanted to push her away, to tell her to leave me alone, that she had seen something private I didn't want anyone to know. Instead, I cried with my face in my hands and struggled to breathe past the massive sobs that tore through me, sobs I had never let myself cry since Drake told me he couldn't remember and I decided I had to be strong for him.

But seeing her there in the hallway had brought it all back, the longing of a little boy for his mother's comforting touch, the need for her to be there during triumphs or failures at school, for her caring hands when I was sick, and for her smile, the same smile that came from eyes that matched my own and told me her rhyme for the clubhouse. The intensity of the pain at her loss was nearly unbearable in that moment.

The pain softened. It was subtle and gentle as the jolt of agony lessened and I felt like I could breathe again. The sharp edges of the memory eased and the thought of her face no longer hurt with each heartbeat. I took a shuddering breath and opened my eyes. I found Dara's gaze. Tears shone on her own cheeks and my sorrow showed in her eyes.

"I never knew the love of a child for a mother could be so special," she said. Her voice broke as more tears trailed down her cheeks.

I shook my head, unable to speak. When I pulled my hand back, Dara let go with an understanding nod. I swallowed and forced myself to say, "It-it's been a long time since I've thought about that day."

"You were so young," she said.

I nodded, collecting myself. "Too young to really understand what was happening then. But for some reason, when I showed it to you, I felt like I lost her all over again." I wiped my face with my sleeve; I then held my sleeve out to her. "Need it?"

She laughed and the musical sound lightened the mood. "I have my own, thank you," she replied. She wiped her face with the hem of her shirt.

We silently regained our composure. I felt embarrassed at crying in front of her. I was about to apologize for it when she said, "I think that's the one thing about being an empath."

I looked at her, but she was staring down at her hands that were now resting in her lap.

"As hard as it is to carry everyone's pain, I get to understand and experience for a brief moment what it feels like to be loved even if it means to experience the pain of losing someone." She looked up at me through lowered lashes. "It really is a gift that you just gave me."

"A gift that made you cry?" I replied. "That's not a very good gift." I lifted a hand and wiped a tear she had missed from her cheek.

She smiled and pushed a strand of my unruly black hair from my forehead. "You continue to surprise me, Finnley Briscoe."

"I hope that a good thing, Dara Jade," I replied, looking down at her.

I had never kissed anyone, but in that moment, staring down into her seemly bottomless violet eyes, I couldn't help myself. I leaned forward and brushed her lips with my own. It was a bold move that surprised me, and somewhere deep inside I felt the approval of my Alpha side. Dara's head tipped up and she kissed me back. It was simple and brief, but enough to make my heart race when I sat back in my chair.

I stared at her. "Dara, I—"

She smiled at me. "You don't have to say anything."

I shook my head slowly. "I don't want you to think I showed you that to gain your sympathy or make you care about me."

She set her hand on my cheek. It was a gentle touch that surprised me. "I would never think that of you, Finn," she said.

I heard another bell ring and started at the reminder that we weren't in our own little world. We had school, a team, and professors who would be waiting for us.

"What?" she asked.

"The bell rang," I replied.

She nodded and rose. "Time for breakfast."

"For first period, I'm afraid," I said apologetically. "The breakfast bell rang a while ago."

She lifted a shoulder. "I can wait until lunch to eat."

I nodded, but I my thoughts were on other things than class.

She must have caught my expression because she asked, "What are you thinking?"

I gestured toward the table. "I need to find that box."

"I'll go with you," she offered.

I shook my head. "It'll be faster if I go alone." Before she could protest, I said, "Besides, I need someone to cover for me here. If the professors start asking, tell them I felt sick and that I'm just trying to sleep it off." A thought occurred to me and I said, "Tell them it's something werewolf related. That'll kill their interest for sure."

Dara rolled her eyes at the suggestion. "You're using their prejudice to your gain."

I shrugged. "Someone should. It might as well be me."

I followed her back up the slide. It was a strange sensation, sliding upward instead of down. It felt as though I pressed rewind on a movie. Climbing back down the invisible staircase was nearly as scary as climbing up. By the time we stepped on the roof, I was grateful for something solid and visible under my feet. "Any chance they made an invisible ledge around this roof in case we fall?" I asked as I balanced my way toward the window.

"Want to be the first to find out?" Dara called over her shoulder.

"No, thank you," I replied with a laugh.

I helped her through the window, then climbed in behind her. It felt nice to set my feet on a solid floor that was neither sloped nor invisible.

The halls were silent as we made our way down the stairs. I paused on the third floor to grab some change and my cellphone.

71

"Be careful, Finn," Dara called as she hurried down toward her class.

"You too," I replied.

I made my way to room C thirty-three and searched through my belongings. "You too?" I muttered to myself. "What does that mean? She told me to be careful and I say, 'You, too?' What, does she need to worry about papercuts or maybe school lunch?" When I thought about my first day at the Academy, I realized there were plenty of dangers Haunted High had to offer. Perhaps telling her to be careful hadn't been too out of line. Still, I thought it was a stupid response.

I couldn't help thinking of our kiss as I pulled on a clean tee-shirt. Dara was the first girl I had ever kissed in my life. If anyone had told me that a sarcastic empath at a haunted high school would be the first person I kissed, I would have thought they were crazy. But standing there with my lips still tingling from the experience was another matter entirely. It was special. Or it was ridiculous. I couldn't decide. Maybe Dara was just being sympathetic. Who wouldn't comfort a werewolf who had just shown the memory of losing his mother. Well, actually I doubted anyone else at the Academy would have cared, but I told myself not to read too much into it.

I shook my head and picked up my wallet. There were only a few dollars inside, but enough to get me home. I took the bills out and shoved them in my pocket. If whatever was in the box really could be a key to the demons, I wasn't sure it was smart to let Dad know about it. My hope was to sneak in and sneak out without anyone knowing I was home. It would be easier that way. My heart tightened at the thought. I shoved it away and headed for the door.

I glanced back once at the ghosts hovering around Alden's bed, waiting for him to return from class. I still wasn't used to them, but until we figured out how to get rid

72

of the demon threat, I knew I didn't have a choice but to tolerate their presence. Alden had tried everything his parents suggested, but still the ghosts hung around. The Grim didn't seem bothered by it, but the students in the hallways gave him and the ghosts a wide berth when they walked by. It wasn't fair to Alden, but he handled it well. He was tougher than anyone gave him credit for.

I took one last look around the room to make sure I hadn't forgotten anything, then pulled the door shut behind me.

One thing to be said about New York is that it wasn't hard to find a bus heading in the direction I needed to go. I made my way to the furthest seat in the back and stared out the window at the buildings and cars rushing by. Though it was slower by bus, it was cheaper than a taxi. With Dad and Julianne at work and Drake at school, I really didn't have other options. I realized I could have used the chance to catch up on some work from class, but I had forgotten my books. Instead, I let my mind wander and listened to the music playing faintly over the radio.

Day changed slowly to night. It wasn't until I felt the tremor run over my skin that I realized I had placed myself in a horrible position. Moonlight filled the bus. Most of the occupants were sleeping as they rode to their final destination. There were only about a dozen of us on the bus at the late hour, and most of them had gotten on when I did. No one else seemed bothered by the light of the moon that streamed plentifully inside.

It had been too long since I phased. I could feel my control slipping. The wolf fought to be free like an itch that quickly turned into a burning need. I knew that if I didn't act soon, I was going to phase in the backseat. I couldn't imagine that the other inhabitants of the bus would react calmly when they realized one of their nameless companions had turned into a wild beast.

My hands shook when I reached up to pull the red line that ran to the front of the bus. As soon as I pulled it, the driver's head jerked up and he studied the occupants of the bus in his overhead mirror. I waved a hand.

"You need to get off?" he said incredulously as he slowed the bus. "There's nothing out here."

I rose and hurried up the aisle toward him. A few of the other bus occupants awoke and glared at me for causing a commotion, but I ignored them with the thought that if I phased in the middle of the aisle, there would be a whole lot more to disturb them.

"This is my stop," I said, practically running past the chairs.

I reached the closed door.

"I don't feel right about letting you out," the bus driver said with an anxious look outside. "It's the middle of the night; only the moon is lighting anything around here right now."

If he mentioned the moon one more time, he was never going to be able to sleep again.

It didn't take much to bring out the Alpha in me. I looked him square in the eyes and said, "Let me out. Now."

I don't know if he saw my eyes turn gold in the half-light of the bus or if my growl was enough to spur him into action, but he opened the door so fast I barely saw his hand move. I climbed outside and turned to say thank you, but the door snapped shut and the bus drove away. I had the distinct sensation that the bus driver couldn't get away fast enough.

Chapter Six

THE MOONLIGHT MADE ME double over in pain. I ducked into the ditch at the side of the road and pulled off my shirt. Shoving my cellphone and the few dollars I had left inside, I tied the sleeves and made a quick pouch. I wished I had thought to bring a long-sleeved shirt or my backpack. I wasn't sure if I could get a backpack on as a wolf, but the thought of arriving at home naked wasn't a pleasant one.

Another pain through my stomach reminded me that I had no choice in the matter anymore. I dropped to my knees and was about to stop fighting when I remembered Sparrow. I quickly held up my hand and touched the dragon gently.

"Sparrow, I need you to wake up little girl. Come on!"

She stirred as I gritted my teeth against the pull of my muscles.

The little dragon yawned and then sleepily unwrapped herself from my wrist.

Fear filled me. I didn't know what the little dragon would do if I phased. I was afraid of scaring her and having her fly off into the darkness. If I lost her after all we had been through together in such a short while, I wouldn't be able to forgive myself. I should have left the dragon with Dara. I knew I sometimes got too wrapped up in what I was dealing with to think outside of a situation, but this time the sylph dragon was the one who could get hurt.

I held her up so that we were at eye level.

"Sparrow, I'm going to phase now. It might be scary, but I want you to wait for me. Don't fly off and get lost out here." I looked around, but we were in the middle of nowhere. I wasn't exactly sure that I could even find my way home, not to mention track down a lost dragon. "Trust me, okay?" I pleaded.

I set her gently on my shirt and moved it to the side so she wouldn't be crushed by accident. The little dragon watched me patiently, her green eyes bright in the moonlight.

I couldn't put it off any longer. I let the pain pull me down and barely remembered to kick off my pants and underwear before the phase took over. My shoulders rolled, my hips rotated, and my bones and muscles shifted. Now that I wasn't fighting it, the phase happened quickly. Black and silver fur ran down my neck and along my back, my ears moved upward and became pointed, and my nose and mouth elongated into a fang-filled muzzle.

When it was over, I shook to let myself get used to the form. I had only phased a few times in my life. It still felt strange to be so close to the ground and stand on four paws. There were benefits, like the fact that I could hear much further away than my human form, and how my sense of smell could identify chickens in the backyard of a house so far away I couldn't see it. I also liked the way my wolf vision turned everything to various shades of gray so that I could see easily in the dark. I also knew where home was. That surprised me. In my human form, I had been worried about finding it, yet as a wolf, I felt which direction it was in without any doubt.

I saw a movement out of the corner of my eye and turned my gaze onto little Sparrow who sat on my tee-shirt. She blinked her purple eyelids over her green eyes. It was the only sign the creature gave of concern over my new form. To keep from scaring her, I lowered onto my belly and inched my nose over to her. To my relief, the dragon merely stepped onto my snout and climbed up my head and between my ears to settle into a place between my shoulder blades. When I glanced back to check on her, I saw that she had already curled into a ball and fallen to sleep. Her claws gripped my fur firmly enough that I saw sure only the roughest of movements would make her budge. With a sigh, she wrapped her black wings around her and let out a breath that preceded sleep.

For lack of any better way to carry it, I grabbed my shirt-wrapped phone in my jaws and began to run.

Running was the best part. It came so easily in wolf form. As my paws stretched out and my muscles pumped, I felt as though I had been born to run my entire life. I set a pace that would have killed me in my other form, and ran for hours with barely a need to slow. It was exhilarating, flying over the ground beside the road, my paws hitting the dirt in a cadence that seemed to match the beat of my heart. I ducked out of the way whenever a vehicle approached, but even then I took joy in the fact that I could lope through the ditch nearly as easily.

I made a game of jumping the roads that crossed the ditch to see if I could make it to the other side. The thought of hurting myself never crossed my mind as my body easily took to the task. I found that if I bunched my muscles and sprang earlier in the run, I could jump lower to the ground and for a further distance. By the time the sun was rising, I felt more at ease in my wolf body. It was nice not worrying about the clutter of human thoughts. As a wolf, it was easy to be in the moment, to relish the run and the feeling of the moonlight on my shoulders. Even the ache of my right paw which had caused me to limp at first moved to the back of my mind.

I reached Cleary as the sun began to rise. The familiarity of the small city made my heart pound. It was cold, with fall just edging on winter, but I didn't feel it through my thick fur. It was strange how we felt locked away from the seasons in the Academy, especially with the strange doors to distant places that didn't seem to feel the seasons as we did. There was ice in a few spots on the road. It brought back memories I didn't want to visit.

I crept through the shadows and made my way behind a grocery store I used to go to all the time with my friends because their soda was cheap and the owner bowled with my dad. I ran through several neighborhoods along the same path I used to travel on my way home from school. I was almost to the cul-de-sac where I lived when I felt the wolf form begin to leave.

No, no, no! I pleaded in my mind with each step. I pushed myself faster, but there was no way I would make it in time. I finally skidded to a stop near Mrs. Thomlinson's house. She still hung her laundry out to dry on a line in the backyard. I knew that because we used to play football in Kendall's yard and lost it a few times over the fence. She hated when we hopped into her yard because she was always afraid we would knock down her carefully strung-out clothes.

I ran through the narrow passage between her house and the side fence, then leaped the gate, grateful I had practiced jumping on my way there. I hit the ground with less grace than I intended. I could already feel my muscles changing form. At the sight of the clothing on the line, I set down the tee-shirt I had carried the entire way and searched quickly through the garments. I found a pair of Mr. Thomlinson's pants and pulled them down. I balked when I turned to the next row and found white briefs far too large for me even if I had considered wearing someone else's underwear, which I would never do.

I carried the pants back to the shadow of the house just in time to beat the phase. I didn't fight it at all this time and was grateful when I made it back to human form easier than ever. The entire phase only took a few minutes. When I was done, I reached carefully back and lifted the sleeping dragon from between my shoulder blades. When I set her on my arm, Sparrow stirred only long enough to wrap around my wrist before she was sleeping again.

"Rough life," I said with a wry smile.

I pulled on the pants and tied the drawstring at the waist. Mr. Thomlinson was a portly man and the drawstring only helped so much, but wearing his pants was far better than the option of no pants at all. I fumbled with my shirt which was torn slightly and had a bit of wolf drool on it from the run. When I pulled it on, I was relieved to find it in at least serviceable condition. I promised myself I would grab some clean clothes from home after I made it inside.

Feeling less conspicuous in my human form and in clothes, I climbed over the gate and made my way toward our house. I hesitated behind the semi-truck parked across the street. I don't know if I had never really expected to reach home or if I figured I would come up with a plan when I did, but sitting there behind the truck with my house only a few steps away made me feel completely unprepared.

The truck brought back a wave of nostalgia. Mr. Dewyze used to let Drake and I sit in the truck on the weekends when he came home. I always imagined driving a semi-truck like that, owning the road and driving wherever I wanted. I knew now that it didn't work like that, truck drivers had bosses to listen to and routes to follow, but when I was younger, driving a truck had seemed like the coolest thing in the world.

I was just about to inwardly thank Mr. Dewyze for parking his truck there that weekend when a footstep caught my ear. I turned and my heart sunk.

"Welcome home, Finnley Briscoe."

I stared up into the face of Sebastian's older brother, Grayson Newton. He had broad shoulders and a football build, but spent most of his time playing videogames when he wasn't working at the grocery store I had just passed. The anger and triumph on his face let me know I had made a very bad mistake.

He grabbed me by the front of my shirt and pinned me up against the truck.

"What do you know?" he said with a sneer. "The prodigal son returns." He paused, then continued with, "Or should I say, prodigal beast?"

I struggled against his hold. I could have broken it easily with my new werewolf strength, but given that his bullying had been a common occurrence before the accident, I thought that it would be better to just go with it.

"Let me down, Grayson," I said.

"Why?" he taunted. "Are you going to bite me?"

I stared at him. "What are you talking about?" Inside, my blood ran cold. I kept my face carefully guarded against revealing how much his words bothered me.

"You know very well what I'm talking about," he replied. "I've seen the pictures. I know what you are and why you weren't at the funeral." He pulled me closer and said with breath that smelled like Doritos, "You're not a very good friend, Finn. You turned into a beast and left my brother there to die. I knew if I waited here long enough, I would catch you and find out the truth for sure."

I was about to deny it all when he said, "Then I'll turn you over to the Maes."

If I felt cold before, my entire body turned to ice at his statement.

He must have seen the flicker of fear on my face because his gaze sharpened. "You know who they are!" he said with triumph in his voice.

Thoughts of the worry on Don Ruvine's face when he told Vicken about his mother filled me. "They're dangerous, Grayson. You need to stay away from them," I told him.

"If you know who they are, then there's more truth to what I'm saying than you're letting on," Grayson replied with a gleam in his eyes that scared me.

I held his gaze. "I have people to protect."

"Your family?" he said. His hands trembled with rage. "Where were you when my family needed protecting? You let Bast die!"

I shook my head. "He was dead when we hit the water." It hurt to relive the memory. The sound of his head striking the window as the car slammed into the water played over and over in my mind. Blood coated Sebastian's face. I shook my head to clear the image.

"You're a liar," Grayson accused. "You let him die there. I know you did."

I shook my head, but I could see in his eyes that he would never believe me. There was only one thing I could do to show him the truth.

"You're not going to like this," I warned.

"Like what?" he asked with such anger I thought he would try to kill me before the Maes could do the job.

"Like this," I replied.

I grabbed his arms with both of my hands and forced the memory at him. Grayson gasped. I pushed mercilessly, shoving the memory at him so that he would be forced to accept that I didn't let his brother die.

He saw us hit the water, saw the way his brother's arms floated in the dark, icy liquid when I left Drake on the bank and returned to save him. I tried to break the window, and felt my breath leave. I heard him draw in a breath in unconscious response to me drowning at the bottom of the lake when I couldn't swim any longer.

I stopped the memory. A brief flicker of triumph filled me at the fact that I had found some control. The elation faded when I opened my eyes and found Grayson staring up at me with tears on his cheeks.

"I-I didn't know," he said. "And how…how did you do that?"

"Put me down first," I told him.

He lowered me back to the ground and let me go. The expression on his face was one of fear mixed with sorrow. A tear fell onto his hand. He looked down at it as if he couldn't figure out where it had come from.

"Come with me, Finn," he said. Without another word, he turned away and left me staring after him.

I was left to debate whether it would be easier just to go inside my house, but the expression on Grayson's face unnerved me. I finally followed him toward their house a few blocks down from ours. As we walked, the sun rose above the edge of the horizon, lighting the quiet neighborhoods with gentle sunshine as though a monster didn't walk in their midst.

"Back here," Grayson called over his shoulder.

I ducked under the loose slat in the fence and trailed behind him to the treehouse us boys had practically grown up in. He motioned for me to follow him up the ladder.

"Grayson, I don't think—"

"Don't think," he called down. "Do." They were the same words he always used to say to Sebastian whenever his brother had a different idea than him. It used to make Sebastian so frustrated; I now understood the feeling.

I couldn't help wondering as I climbed up the rope ladder if I was going willingly into some sort of trap. My instincts thrummed and I checked the air, but couldn't smell that anyone other than Grayson had been up the ladder in a long time. Sebastian's lingering scent made my heart ache. I gritted my teeth and pulled myself up to the top.

I paused at the edge of the treehouse hatch and stared. Pinned to the walls and covering the table we had made from an orange crate were charts, pictures from the accident, a map with different colors of pins in it that led to partially-obscure pictures of monsters, and several drawings and notes on werewolf characteristics.

"Grayson, what is this?" I asked in quiet horror.

"Logistics," he replied, his eyes wide and wild. "Everyone needs logistics. That way I can impress the Monster Abolition and Eradication Society."

I shook my head. "You don't want to impress them. They're monster killers."

"You're a monster who's a killer," Grayson replied.

I looked into his unstable gaze and said, "You saw what I showed you. The accident was from ice across the bridge. Sebastian died in the fall. N-not by my hands." I couldn't help the way my voice broke. Seeing it again had shaken me, and to hear the accusation in Grayson's voice gripped my heart in a fist.

"You're the reason he's dead," Grayson said with a hitch in his words. "If he hadn't been with you, he'd be here today." He shook his head and made a wild wave of his hand. "It doesn't matter. What matters is that there are monsters out there like you who need to be stopped before they hurt anyone else." He turned his back on me and studied the charts before him.

"Like here. Reports say a girl was attacked in an alley in Venton. When she was found, she was taken to a hospital with bite marks on her neck and no memory of what happened." He pointed to another line where a green string ran from a small town to a blurry picture of a sasquatch. "And here, there have been tons of sightings of a Big Foot. People are afraid to camp because they think the smell of hotdogs and marshmallows will attract him to their camp." His finger thumped on a picture of murky water. "And don't get me started on the merman of Johnson Lake. Even I could find him given all the rumors."

"Why would you want to?" I asked.

He stared at me. "Because they're dangerous."

"How?"

He opened his mouth, closed it again, then opened it and said, "Because they're monsters, Finn!" He spun back to his pictures.

I watched him carefully, uncertain of what I should do. "What about me?"

"You should go."

Relief swept through me. "I can leave?"

He glanced over his shoulder. "If you didn't show me what you did, I'd be taking you in to the Maes right now." His voice lowered and he said, "I know you cared about Sebastian. You were a good friend. But be careful. I'm not the only one who's been suspicious about you and your family."

I had to force myself to ask, "Will you try to join the Maes still?"

Darkness swept through his gaze. "We have to stop the monsters, Finn. They're dangerous. I won't stop until they're gone."

I climbed down the ladder with a heavy feeling of foreboding on my shoulders. My plan to sneak in and out of my house had vanished in the face of the threat Grayson brought up. I tried the front door, but it was locked. I could have rung the doorbell, but the thought of doing it at my own house rankled the last of my pride that hung threadbare since wearing somewhere else's pants became my last option for sneaking through my own city.

I unlatched the gate and walked around back. I paused at the edge of the grass. There was something calming about standing in the yard I had grown up in. The tall wooden fence we helped Dad stain every year was surrounded by fruit trees that felt like old friends. Drake and I had climbed them since we could walk. We had apple wars, picked cherries, and had eaten so many apricots one year we got sick. The trees had been our shade for family picnics, and were the bane of our existence when we had to rake leaves in the fall. Dad always looked the other way when we spent more time jumping in the piles than doing a good job.

The grass was getting long. I wondered if it hurt Dad's thumb to mow it. I should ask Drake to take over. There were piles of lumber next to the back door where Dad had started the deck. The holes filled with cement and supports gave me an idea of how big it was going to be. It made me smile to think of Dad being finally able to build the deck he had always dreamed of. I made a vow to help him complete it during our holiday time off.

My smile faded when I turned to see the scene in through the back door. Dad, Julianne, and Drake sat around the kitchen table eating breakfast. Julianne said something and both Drake and Dad laughed. They looked so happy there, Julianne with her hand on her belly that looked even bigger than before I left, Drake with his hair disheveled; he held his bacon in one hand and used it to scoop eggs onto his toast in the other even though Julianne always scolded him about using a fork. Dad had on his favorite red and black striped shirt and the black tie he said was his lucky teaching tie. His students must have a test today. He always wore it to give them the best chance at passing.

I didn't want to break up their carefree breakfast. The scent of eggs, bacon, and Julianne's homemade sourdough toast made my mouth water. I couldn't remember the last time I had eaten. I was about to turn away when Julianne looked up. Her eyes met mine and widened. A smile crossed her face. She said something to Drake and Dad and they both looked me.

"Finn!" Drake said.

Dad motioned for me to come in. When I hesitated, Drake jumped up and pulled the door open.

"I didn't want to interrupt," I said lamely.

To my surprise, Drake hugged me. "It's good to have you home," my brother said.

I stepped inside to the embraces of Dad and Julianne.

My stepmother chided me even while she hugged me. "You should have called. We could have picked you up!"

"In hindsight, it would have been easier," I admitted. "I didn't plan to disturb you guys."

She stepped back to look at me and gave me a warm smile. "You're part of this family, Finn. You know you're always welcome here." Her eyebrows pulled together as she looked me up and down. "You're not eating enough. Come on. I made plenty."

I tried to protest, but she herded me to the table and had set a plate heaping with food in front of me before I could get a word in.

Dad squeezed my shoulder on his way back to his seat. "Good to have you home, son," he said.

"Where'd you get those pants?" Drake asked. "They look like something Mr. Thomlinson would wear."

That made me laugh. "They are Mr. Thomlinson's actually." At their surprised looks, embarrassment filled me. "I took the bus here and couldn't make it home with the moonlight." It felt so weird to talk to them about being a werewolf. I didn't know how much Dad had told Julianne, but when I looked at her, she gave an understanding nod. "So I had to get off the bus before I phased in front of everyone."

"That would have made the news, I'm sure," Drake said with a laugh.

I grinned. "Yeah. I figured I'd try to keep a low profile. So when I reached Cleary, I realized when I phased back that I wouldn't have any clothes."

"So you pilfered Mr. Thomlinson's," Dad said. "I'll slip some money in their mailbox to pay for the pants."

"Thanks," I told him. "I didn't plan on stealing them." I pointed to my dirty shirt. "I carried this in my mouth."

Drake laughed so hard he nearly fell off his chair. "I wish I could have seen that!" he said. "A big scary wolf carrying his shirt in his fangs!"

I took a bite of the eggs. I had forgotten how good Julianne's cooking was. "This is amazing," I told her.

"It's just eggs," she replied. "If you let us know you're coming next time, I'll make a real treat."

"Why did you come here?" Dad asked. His tone was light to make the question unaccusatory, but the curiosity on his face was undeniable.

I let out a breath and admitted, "The Academy's in trouble, and so are we."

Chapter Seven

"WHAT DO YOU MEAN, we're in trouble?" Julianne asked.

I told them quickly about my encounter with Grayson.

"So he knows," Dad said with a nod. "I've seen him sneaking around a few times and was afraid he believed the stories of you being some kind of monster."

"They're not stories," I reminded him. "And with the videos whoever saw the accident took, I don't know how I can deny it." I shook my head as anger filled me. "Who films an accident instead of helping out anyway? They're the real monsters."

Dad set a hand on my arm. "Alright, Finn. It's okay. We'll figure out a way to take care of it. But for now, I'm glad you're safe. At least Grayson didn't call the Maes."

"Who's the Maes?" Drake asked.

89

I could see the same question on Julianne's face. I figured they had a right to know since everyone was in danger thanks to my slipup.

"The Monster Abolition and Eradication Society," I told them. "They're monster hunters, basically. According to Professor Briggs, they travel the world hunting down and killing anyone they think is a monster." I looked at Drake. "Do you remember the mean vampire from the Academy?"

He nodded.

"That's Don Ruvine. He's the head of the nation's vampire coven and the father of one of my classmates." I almost called Vicken a friend, but that would have been a very long stretch. I went on with, "The Don's wife was captured by the Maes. They're expecting some sort of demand, but they haven't heard back. His daughter was also taken by demons while she was at the Academy."

"They have really bad luck," Drake said.

Dad shook his head. "No wonder he was in such a bad mood. I shouldn't have goaded him."

"You goaded a vampire?" Julianne said with horror in her voice.

I shook my head. "Dad was fine. He was just trying to defend me. Werewolves aren't exactly welcome at the Academy."

"But isn't that why we sent you there?" Julianne said, trying to understand. "You're supposed to be safer at that school and now I'm hearing about demons kidnapping people and vampires who have some sort of a vendetta against werewolves? That doesn't sound very safe to me."

I gave her my most reassuring smile. "I need to be there, Juli. Trust me. It's a good place." I let the worry I felt show. "But something evil is trying to hurt the students and I think I've found the key to figure out what it is. That's why I came here." I looked at Dad. "Is it ok if I go through Mom's boxes in the attic?"

Surprise showed on his face, but he nodded. "Of course. Whatever you need."

I took a few more bites of food. It was easier to relax after telling them everything. At least I didn't feel like I was holding such heavy secrets. I smiled as I listened to the small talk. Drake's goal of beating all of my records in track sounded like it was going well. As much as I hated seeing my name booted down the list, I was glad my brother was the one doing it. Dad had a few students in his science class who needed to take school a bit more seriously; he wasn't looking forward to his upcoming parent-teacher conference. Julianne was working part-time at the fabric store until her doctor put her on mandatory leave, though her boss was worried her water would break on the store floor any day now.

I had reached for my cup of orange juice when Julianne said, "Finn, what's on your hand?"

I was worried at first that she had seen my palm. I had been careful to keep my right hand under the table until I could rewrap it. Maybe she noticed that I wasn't eating with my dominant hand. But when I followed her gaze, I realized she was looking at the sleeping dragon.

A smile crossed my face. "This is Sparrow." I turned my wrist over so she could see the little creature.

"She's amazing," Drake breathed. "You need to see her fly." He leaned so far over the table he nearly tipped his cup of orange juice over to get a better view.

"She's a real dragon?" Julianne asked in surprise.

I nodded. "I showed Sparrow to Dad and Drake at the Academy, but I thought you would like to see her. Watch."

I brought my wrist up and ran a finger down the dragon's back. "Sparrow, do you want to wake up? I have someone for you to meet."

A gasp sounded from my stepmother when the little dragon lifted her black and purple head and gave a yawn.

"She is so precious!" Julianne said.

"She's incredible," Drake agreed.

Dad's voice showed his awe when he said, "It was so amazing when Finn showed it to us at the Academy. I forgot to tell you about the dragon with everything else that happened at the school. I felt like I was in some sort of dream the whole time I was there."

I turned my hand over and Sparrow walked to my palm. She shook and straightened out her wings.

"And man can she fly!" Drake said.

A buzz caught my ear. I spotted a fly swarming around the overhead light.

"Sparrow, are you hungry?" I asked the dragon. I lifted her so she could see the fly.

"Yes!" Julianne exclaimed. "I've been trying to swat that one all morning!"

The instant Sparrow caught sight of the bug, she sprang from my hand and darted after it. Everyone watched with awe on their faces as the dragon circled the fly and then pounced. She brought it back to the table and landed lightly next to my plate. The sound of her crunching up the fly warred with my appetite.

Drake couldn't take his eyes off her. "That was so cool!" he said.

"Neat," Julianne agreed with a nod. "Next time we have a fly problem, I'm calling you home."

"Deal," I said with a grin.

Dad carefully put out his hand. "Can I pet her?" he asked. "I don't want to hurt her."

"You can pet her," I said. I showed him how to run his finger down her back so her spikes didn't poke him. "She loves it."

As if in response to my words, the little dragon lifted her back like a cat so she could be petted more. My dad smiled and ran his fingers down her spikes. When he sat back in his chair, the little dragon pranced closer to him. His smile turned into a pleased grin and he continued to pet her.

"Finn, what happened to your hand?" Julianne asked.

I realized I had reached for my fork with my right hand by habit. I turned it over and heard my stepmom gasp.

"What happened?" she exclaimed.

"Finn, you said it was nothing," Dad said with a stern expression.

"You knew about it?" Julianne asked him.

Dad nodded. "His friend told me he got burned in class, but Finn told me later he hurt it stopping a demon that attacked the school." His brow furrowed as he looked at the wound. "But he made me believe it wasn't bad." He shot me an accusing look.

I had to admit that it looked horrible. Running on my paw hadn't done the burn any good. The black edges that curled away from the throbbing red center of my palm gave it a dramatically nasty appearance. I had to admit that it hurt pretty much as bad as it looked, and possibly even worse now that I saw it.

"Someone had to stop the demon. It was trying to kill a student. So I acted," I said.

It sounded far more heroic than it had been. My instincts had spurred me to react. Bowling over the demon and holding it down despite the flames may have been foolish in hindsight, but it was all I could think of to do. The thought of Claria Fig sleeping soundly in the infirmary made me feel a bit better about my actions.

"Doesn't your school have some sort of protection against things like that?" Julianne asked. "I mean, I don't know how it works there, but it sounds like you need it."

I pulled my hand back without telling her that my team was the protection.

"I'm hoping we won't need it if I find what I'm looking for," I told her instead. "Maybe we can end the threat without anyone else being at risk."

"You, especially," she replied. "Let me bandage that up before you get an infection."

I followed her to the kitchen counter and she began to pull the medical supplies from the cupboard she kept overly stocked for just such an event.

"It was wrapped before I phased," I said sheepishly. "I honestly didn't think about it after that."

She paused with the antiseptic in her hand. "So, um...." She stopped as though she didn't know what to say.

"What?" I probed. "You can ask me anything."

A hint of red colored her cheeks and she looked down at the ointment in her hand. "Your dad told me all about the werewolf stuff and showed me the picture of your mother, but...well...."

I stared at her and a smile touched my face. "Do you want to see what I look like as a wolf?"

"It's stupid of me to ask, I know," she said quickly. "You don't have to. You just came a long way and—"

"No," I said, lifting my good hand. "It's fine, really. You've always been there for us and you had no idea what you were getting into."

"To be fair, neither did you," Julianne pointed out.

I smiled. "Yeah. But I need to get out of these clothes anyway. I'll be back."

I turned to find Dad and Drake watching me from the table. Dad's fingers still ran down Sparrow's back. The little dragon had curled up on his napkin and appeared quite content with the pampering.

"I'll admit that I'm interested to see what you look like as a wolf," Dad said with a hint of embarrassment in his voice.

"Yeah," Drake said. "The last time you nearly scared me to death. I'm hoping you're a little less terrifying looking in the light, not wet, and not during the most horrible moment of my life."

I felt embarrassed by all the attention. "Yeah, okay," I said with forced nonchalance. "I'll be back."

I hesitated in the kitchen doorway and glanced at Julianne. "But don't hit me with the broom," I told her.

She laughed and Dad chuckled. "Don't worry. I'll put it away," she reassured me.

When we went camping last year, a dog from one of the other campgrounds had found his way into our cooler of food. No amount of yelling or scare tactics made the animal leave until Julianne got out the broom from Dad's truck. It was our family joke that she could handle any intruder with it.

I jogged up the stairs to my room and paused just inside the door. I don't know why I had expected it to change, but everything had stayed exactly where I had left it. I could tell Julianne had vacuumed by the tracks on the carpet, but she had gone around the sock I left near the door. I think it was their way of letting me know that the room would always be mine. The sentiment was touching, but at the same time, it felt like a ghost lived in the room instead of me.

I sat down on the bed and looked around. The clothes in the closet, the track trophies on the dresser, and the game system in the corner seemed like something from a dream. I had been the guy in the picture on the dresser who flipped backwards off the boat Dad had rented at the lake. In the next photo, a group of our friends, Sebastian included, sat on the bleachers shouting at the high school football game. Everyone looked so carefree and happy. My gaze lingered on Bast's smiling face before I turned my gaze away.

I reminded myself that my family was waiting for me. They expected me to phase. I was just glad they didn't know how long it took.

I pulled off my borrowed pants. At least phasing was an excuse to get out of them and into something I actually owned. I pulled off my shirt as well and tossed them in the hoop that dropped to the hamper below my window. At the last minute, I remembered to grab my cellphone out of my pants pocket and shove it in the jeans I planned to wear back to school.

Standing there naked in the middle of my room waiting for the phase to come felt like perhaps the most awkward moment of my life. I didn't know how to start the phase. Vicken's words repeated in my mind from when I had told him as much during my attempt to track down his sister after she disappeared.

'You can't just make it happen? Doesn't that make you dangerous?' he had asked.

I may be dangerous, but I was determined to find some control for my werewolf state. The problem was that I didn't know if it was possible. There weren't any other werewolves I could ask. But I had to assume, at least for my sanity, that control was possible.

I let out a slow breath and counted to ten to clear my head. I thought of how it had felt to be a wolf last night, to run through the ditches and along the road with a freedom unlike anything I had ever felt before. I thought of the wind through my fur and the smell of the chickens in the yard I couldn't see. My fingers began to tingle as I thought of the night with a variety of grays so beautiful I felt as though I had never really seen the night with my human eyes.

The phase pulled me to my knees, but it was milder than I expected. Instead of aching pain at the changing of my limbs, the discomfort was mild as the fur grew, my bones shifted location, and my body accepted the form of the wolf. I didn't know if it was because this was the first time I had ever chosen to become a wolf, or if it was easier since I didn't fight it from the beginning, but the end of the phase found me standing comfortably on all fours in my bedroom.

The sock near the door stunk. I snorted and fought back the urge to pick it up in my mouth and put it in the hamper. There were just some things I refused to do as a wolf. With such a long tongue, the dirty sock flavor would probably never leave.

I was grateful I had forgotten to close the door completely. Howling and scratching at it like a common dog so that Julianne would hear me and open it would destroy the last shred of self-respect I had. Instead, I was able to carefully maneuver my claws into the crack and pull it open wide enough that I could shove it aside with my nose. I padded into the hallway and then down the stairs.

"What a cute little dragon," Julianne was saying. "Do you think we could talk Finn into leaving her here? She'd be very safe."

"That'd be awesome," Drake said. "Then I could take her to school and show all of my friends.

I winced when I stepped on the third from the bottom stair and it creaked the way it always did.

"I think he's coming," I heard Dad tell them.

Everyone grew quiet.

I paused at the edge of the doorway. My heart thundered in my chest almost as badly as it had the night I fought the demon. I grinned at my own foolish nerves, and then stopped grinning because I realized if I came into the kitchen like that they might think I was a snarling, wild wolf unable to control myself and be truly terrified.

I took a calming breath and padded forward.

"Oh, Finn," Julianne breathed with a smile on her face. "You're beautiful!"

I snorted. Being beautiful was the last thing I had expected to hear.

"You do look really cool," Dad told me. "I, uh, can you understand us?"

I gave a short nod.

"Cool!" Drake exclaimed. He dropped to his knees in front of me. "Can you come to school with me? I could tell everyone I have a trained wolf for a pet. You could do tricks and—"

"Drake," Dad cut him off. "Calm down. Your brother has to go back to school. He doesn't have time to pretend to be your pet."

He shot me a smile as if aware of how strange the conversation was.

"Do you have to brush your fur?" Julianne asked.

"Really?" Dad said. "That's what you ask him?"

"What?" she replied self-consciously. "It's a good question. That's a lot of fur to care for and it's obvious how healthy it is." She ran her fingers through the fur at the back of my neck. "It's probably great for how cold it's getting outside. Though I'll bet you shed a lot come summer."

I snorted again and backed up.

"Oh, right. You should go change back so I can bandage your hand," she said with a pointed look at my paw. It hurt to put my weight on it. Apparently running so far hadn't exactly been good on the wound that refused to heal.

"It's only one day, Finn," Drake urged. "You can come to school with me today, scare all of my friends, and then go back to your school tomorrow."

"Drake," Dad warned.

Drake pointed at the dragon who was still preening under the attention Dad was giving her. "Then how about I borrow the dragon? I wouldn't get her taken away; I promise."

Unable to respond, I turned and trotted back up the stairs to my room. Phasing back was even easier. I attributed it to the fact that the moon wasn't out. It took only a few seconds of thinking about pulling on clean clothes for my body to give up the wolf form and transition into that of being human.

I grabbed my favorite black long-sleeved shirt that was worn enough to be comfortable but could still pass as fairly tidy, and pulled on underwear and then my pants. I wondered if it would be possible to find the pants I had left behind, but the time it would take to find exactly where the bus had dropped me off wasn't worth it. Maybe someone who needed them would find my old pair of jeans and be grateful for them. Perhaps they would also burn the underwear.

I mourned the loss of my shoes even more. They were the second pair I had lost from turning into a werewolf. The first, my new pair of sneakers, lay at the bottom of the river from the accident. The pair I had lost last night were my favorite running shoes. I grudgingly pulled on the old pair of sneakers I wore when I mowed the lawn. If I kept it up, I would be living in dollar flip-flops in order to keep from going broke buying shoe replacements.

When I reached the kitchen again, I found that Julianne had already tidied up. She had also made an extra sack lunch.

"Just in case you want something to eat on the way home," she explained at my look. "Since your dad can't get out of teaching today, I'm going to go into work and see if I can get my shift changed around so I can drive you back. I hate to think of you on the bus by yourself all that way."

I gave her a hug. "I appreciate it," I told her. "And I really am fine on the bus. If it doesn't work out, it's the thought that counts."

She patted my back. When I stepped away, I caught the surprised look she threw my dad at my unusual show of gratitude. I knew hugging wasn't usually my thing, but her kindness after everything that had happened at the Academy was like a breath of fresh air.

"Thank you," she replied. "Now let's see that hand."

I set my right hand on the counter obediently.

She shook her head. "It doesn't look good, Finn."

I nodded. "The doctor at Haunted High said it's going to take a while to heal." I didn't add that he said wounds from demon fire might never heal completely.

"I'm glad you have a doctor there," she said as she spread ointment across the wound. She looked up at me. "Does everyone call the Academy Haunted High?"

I nodded. "The students do, and a lot of the professors. Especially lately."

"I heard about the ghosts," she told me. "It's a little hard to picture without being there."

I shot Dad a look. He answered my unspoken question with a shake of his head. He had apparently kept the appearance of my mother's ghost to himself. I couldn't blame him. Since nobody knew exactly what was happening with the ghosts at the Academy, it was probably the easier choice. I wouldn't have known how to put seeing Mom into words either.

She set a pad of gauze over the middle of my hand and then proceeded to wrap it snuggly with more gauze. She then tied the gauze across the back of my hand and snipped the ends close so they wouldn't snag on anything.

"This should hold until you have to change form again," she said. She began to put the supplies back, then hesitated. "Should I send some of these with you?"

I shook my head. "The infirmary at the Academy has it all. Dr. Six said I can use whatever I need."

Drake perked up. "Why is he named Doctor Six? Does he have six tentacles or maybe six hands?"

I shook my head. "I think it's just her last name. She's a short witch who works with crystals to heal along with the regular stuff." At his disappointed look, I added, "But she wears a top hat and glasses with gears on them."

"Cool," he said, apparently satisfied that she met his requirement for a physician at such a strange school.

Dad rose from the table. "I'd like to stay, but I have class," he said apologetically. He nudged Drake on his way past. "So do you."

"Can I help Finn find what he's looking for? I promise to walk straight to school afterwards," my brother begged.

I met Dad's gaze and lifted a shoulder. "I could probably use the help," I said, gesturing with my hand. The truth was that I wasn't ready to say goodbye to everyone yet. A little more time with my brother was more than welcome.

Dad must have read my expression because he gave in. "Very well." He speared Drake with a stern look. "But head to school right after."

"I promise," Drake said.

"I need to head to work, too," Julianne told us. She kissed my cheek. "If I'd known you were coming, I would have taken the morning off instead of the afternoon."

"It's alright," I told her. "I didn't give you guys a head's up. I'll let you know next time."

"I'm just hoping it's soon," she said, giving me a hug and then Dad and Drake. "It's nice having you home."

Dad nodded. "Definitely. We've missed you around here." His voice grew solemn and he said, "We'll figure things out, Finn. You don't have to hide your whole life, I promise."

I gave him a hug. "I know. It'll work out."

I crossed to the table and held out my hand to Sparrow who still sat on Dad's napkin watching us. The dragon crawled onto my hand and curled around my wrist.

"Is that where she sleeps?" Dad asked.

I nodded. "She's just a baby, so she spends a lot of time sleeping. This is the most I've seen her awake since she hatched."

"She hatched. That's cool," Drake said.

I rolled my eyes. "Let's go start looking."

Dad and Julianne headed for the door. "Be careful where you put your feet up there. You don't want to fall through the sheetrock," Dad reminded us.

"Will do," I promised.

Chapter Eight

DRAKE AND I DUG through the boxes in the attic until we reached the one in the very back. My heart skipped a beat when I saw the demon sigil drawn on the front in black permanent marker.

"What's that?" Drake asked.

"The sign I was looking for," I replied. I didn't want to tell him about Chutka the Shambler or the other terrors that might arise from the demon's presence.

"Open it," Drake urged.

I paused with my hands on the box. My hesitation came from the way the box had been closed. The other boxes had their top flaps folded together in the customary way so that the last flap was forced under the first to close it. This one, however, had been sealed with so much tape even the edges were covered in it. I looked around for something to use, but the attic was severely lacking in sharp, pointed objects.

"Let's take it downstairs," I suggested.

Drake followed me down the steps. The fifteen-year-old had regarded me differently since I had phased into a wolf. There was a quietness to his demeanor as if he was thinking over everything we had gone through. Several times while we searched the attic I had held up a box only to find him watching me and studying me instead of what I was doing.

When I set the box on the table, I turned to find the same expression on his face.

"What?" I asked, keeping my tone light.

Drake blinked. "What?" he replied.

I kept my voice patient when I said, "You keep looking at me. What are you thinking?"

Drake looked at the box, the table, the floor, and then at me again. When he saw that I wasn't going to move until he gave me an answer, he sighed. "I just keep wondering."

"What do you wonder?"

He cringed when he said, "I wonder which part of you is the wolf part."

I lifted an eyebrow.

He quickly rushed forward to say, "You're really a wolf, you know? When I think back to that night, the memory is all blurry and I don't really know what I saw. But here, in the kitchen, you were really a wolf, all fur and teeth and pointed ears and everything. I just...I just wonder where it all goes when it's not you."

I let out a breath. "It's still inside me. I can feel it."

I sat down at the table.

"You can feel it?" Drake prompted.

I nodded. I wasn't sure how much to tell him, but since Mom hadn't shared anything from that life with us, I felt like whatever I could tell him might help him be prepared in case in happened to him someday.

"I feel it if I get mad, or if the moonlight is bright. Sometimes when danger is near I feel this tremor as if my instincts are warning me about it." It was hard to put how I felt into words. I tried anyway. "Sometimes it's like if I don't maintain perfect control, I'm going to lose it and the wolf will take over." I debated if that was enough to tell them, but I couldn't stop myself from saying, "The Headmistress at Haunted High says I'm an Alpha. That's some sort of werewolf leader."

Drake grinned. "Cool."

I lifted a shoulder. "Sometimes it is, but I find myself arguing with my professors—"

"You?" Drake said incredulously.

I nodded. "I can't help it. And if someone is in trouble, I feel like I have to protect them, even if it's the last thing I do."

Drake's voice was quiet when he said, "Like with the demon?"

I followed his gaze to my wrapped hand. "Yeah, like with the demon."

Silence filled the room for a moment before Drake broke it to say, "I was mad about that."

His words surprised me. "About the demon?"

He nodded. "You could have been killed. Even though you didn't say it, I saw it on your face when you told Juli and Dad about it. You saved that student, but you could have been killed." He ran a hand across the worn tabletop and concluded without meeting my gaze, "You should have thought of us."

I wanted to argue with him that I had acted in the heat of the moment or that the Alpha side of me spurred me forward, but it wasn't the answer he needed to hear. I had left my younger brother to go to a school that he now knew was full of monsters and danger in a life where hunters tracked us down and tried to kill us.

I gave the answer he needed to hear. "Drake, I promise I will think about you, Dad, Julianne, and the baby before I do anything dangerous like that again."

"You promise?" he asked, holding my guess with hope on his face.

I nodded.

To my surprise, my younger brother jumped up and gave me a hug. It wasn't that we weren't a hugging family. My dad, mom, and Julianne never spared their hugs or kisses as we grew up. Yet the older we got, the fewer signs of affection my brother and I shared. It took me a second to collect myself and return the hug.

"Alright, enough of this mushy stuff," I said to lighten the mood.

Drake laughed and stepped back. "Let's open this box," he declared.

We used Julianne's scissors to cut the tape. I took a steeling breath and pulled the flaps apart. Our anticipation faded at the sight of the single wooden box sitting in the bottom. I couldn't explain why it hadn't rattled around when I was carrying the carboard box, but it sat in the dead center. I picked it up and looked it over. The box was made of some sort of stained dark wood. The joints were roughly joined together and didn't meet up well. A keyhole showed on one side; other than that, there were no other marks, not even the mark of Chutka.

"That's a letdown," Drake said, eyeing the box with disappointment on his face.

"Yeah, really," I replied. I tried to pry it open, but quickly gave up. If the lid did yield, I preferred it to be at the

Academy where people were prepared to deal with what we found. Hopefully.

"You should probably head to school," I told Drake. "I'll text you to let you know I made it back safe."

"Alright, I—"

My cellphone rang and I jumped. I couldn't remember ever hearing it ring before. I pulled it out of my pocket and smiled at Julianne's name.

"Hi, Juli," I said.

"Hey, Finn, guess what?" Before I could guess, she rushed on to say, "I got someone to cover my shift so I can take you back to the Academy! That way you don't have to ride the bus. It'll be easier and your dad's all for it."

"Really?" I replied, touched by the effort she had taken. "That would be great. Thanks!"

"See you in five," she said before hanging up.

Drake headed for the door.

"Keep an eye out for Grayson," I reminded him.

"Don't worry," he replied, pausing with his hand on the doorknob. "We'll be careful. Just promise me you'll do the same."

I nodded and he grinned before he shut the door behind him.

The drive back to the Academy was in a far more comfortable vehicle than the bus. I had been dreading the risk of taking the bus again only to find the same bus driver driving. I had no idea how I would answer his questions about what had happened when he dropped me off in the middle of nowhere at night and how I had made it to Cleary. Julianne had saved me without knowing it.

However, I was in another uncomfortable situation that may have been worse depending on how I looked at it. Juli always meant well. She was perhaps the nicest person in the entire world. I had seen her bend over backwards cooking

107

until midnight to finish items for a bake sale when one of the mothers at school didn't get enough volunteers. But because of that, she was also reluctant to tell anyone something negative. I had a feeling I knew why she had volunteered to drive me.

I listened to Julianne sing to the radio. Her voice may not have been on par or even close to those on the air, but she didn't care. Sometimes the lyrics she sang didn't match the real words of the songs, but I always enjoyed her carefree way of singing that usually made the entire family join in. After about an hour of listening, I cleared my throat.

"Um, Juli?"

She glanced at me. "Yes, Finn?"

I looked out the window for a moment as I debated how to say what I needed to. I shifted uncomfortably in my seat, then went with, "I really can stay at the Academy."

My thoughts went to Dara and how hard it must have been on her to see all of the students with their families on parent night while she had no one.

"What are you talking about?" Julianne asked with a concerned expression.

I lifted a shoulder and said, "I completely understand if having me around makes it too dangerous for you, Dad, Drake, and the new baby." I gestured toward her stomach that barely fit beneath the steering wheel. "I wouldn't want me around." The words came out tighter than I intended. I hadn't expected my throat to close as I said them. I cleared my throat again and looked away from her searching gaze.

"Finn, darling, I don't want you to stay away from home," she began, alternating between looking at me and the road.

"Isn't that why you offered to drive me?" I asked. "So you could talk to me in private?" At her horrified expression, I rushed on to say, "Not that I blame you. I really don't. I don't think the baby is safe around me, and if Drake doesn't turn out to be a werewolf, you can raise the baby without worry that someone like Grayson is going to pop up armed and with a vendetta against monsters."

Julianne had turned the radio down when I started to talk; I found myself wishing she would turn it back up to drown out the silence that pounded relentlessly against my ears.

"You're our boy, Finn," Julianne started slowly. Her gaze was on the road, but I could see her eyes crease at the corners as she thought aloud. "There is nothing that would keep you from coming home to us, not some monster hunter society, not you turning into an animal," she glanced at me, "Not even if you were stuck as a wolf and couldn't turn back."

A shiver ran down my spine at the thought.

She went on, oblivious to how her words had set me on edge, "You are this baby's big brother, and he or she needs you in his or her life. You'll be there even if I have to pick you up at that school and drag you home."

The thought made me chuckle and broke the tension. "You're sure?" I asked, glancing at her sideways.

"Of course I'm sure!" she replied. "This family isn't a family without you."

Her words meant the world to me. I couldn't smother the smile that stayed on my face as I watched the hilly country turn slowly into the busy city. Eventually, Julianne turned the radio back up. It was a song we both loved. I looked at her and found her watching me with an expectant expression. I laughed and belted out the chorus at the top of my lungs. She joined me opera-style and together we proceeded to shame any stray yowling alley cat who happened to hear us drive past.

When she dropped me off at school, I walked up to the gate alone. Before I could press the button on the box at the side to state my name, the gate swung slowly open. I gave it a searching glance when I passed, but couldn't see the reason for the welcome, even if it was slightly foreboding given the late hour. I waved at Julianne and watched her drive away before I headed inside.

Instead of going to my room and falling into bed like I probably should have, I made sure nobody was in sight, then ducked behind the unicorn photograph at the end of the corridor. With the box in hand, I hurried down the stairs to the basement.

Nobody was there, but they must have just left if the fire burning low in the fireplace was any indication. Knives sat along the far end of the table, revealing that Mercer had begun weapons' practice with the vampires. I set the box in the middle of the table, then carried a few candles over to the fireplace to light. I set a candelabra close to the box and studied it.

By the end of another hour, I had to admit that there was no way to open it without the key. Even throwing it against the wall or trying to burn it in a desperate attempt to figure out what was inside left the box eerily unscathed. I attempted one last time to pry it open with my werewolf strength, then finally gave up, my heart thundering and my fingers aching from the effort. I set the box on the table again and studied my hand.

The bandages had pulled back from my palm with the exertion and the wound didn't look any better than it had at home. The fact that demon fire had damaged me to such an extent made me nervous. I knew such nerves could be the death of me and my team. If I was afraid to face a demon because of demon fire, there was no way I could save Amryn and no way to protect my team against further threat. I had to face my fears.

For lack of a better option, I approached Mercer's box in the far corner. I carried it to the table, then, using the same care he had demonstrated, I took out the black candlestick holder the man had used when he first revealed the flame. I then opened the smaller box inside the big one. The green flame of the imitation demon fire sprang to life the moment the candle met the air. Using the tongs set inside the box for that reason, I gently lifted the candle and set it on top of the dark wood. The green light reached eagerly into the air far higher than a normal flame would have. I put the box away and then stared at the fire. My mouth felt dry.

"I can beat this," I said aloud.

I shoved my left hand into the flame, careful not to let it lap low enough to awaken Sparrow. The agony of fire touching my skin made me clench my other hand into a fist. I used the pain of my damaged palm to center myself and let out a breath. I told myself that I was in control, that the burning I felt was just an illusion. The demon fire couldn't hurt me if I didn't lose concentration. As long as I believed it wasn't melting my skin, the fire had no power.

But the pain was excruciating. I felt the minute details of my skin burning through, of the marrow of my bones beginning to simmer, and of my muscles and tendons peeling back from the wound. My hand shook and I fought to keep it there as long as I could. I counted my heartbeats as I watched the flame lap through my hand the way it had done when I fought the demon. I sucked in another breath, held it for ten heartbeats, then let it out and pulled my hand back.

Relief filled me when the hole that had burned through my skin vanished and the flesh appeared intact once more. I moved my fingers to remind myself that the fire had no power over me. But it wasn't my left hand I was worried about. If a demon attacked, I needed to be able to use both hands to defend myself. If I couldn't, I would put every life at risk and I would have no chance of freeing Amryn.

I let out a slow breath and stuck my right hand over the flame. The green fire immediately ate through the bandages covering my hand. I bit back a cry as the pain doubled. My knees threatened to give way. I leaned against the table, determined to do better than a few seconds. Sweat beaded on my forehead as the scent of burning flesh tangled in my nostrils. My fingers shook and soon my hand and then my arm followed. It was all I could do to tell myself that the fire didn't affect me. Tears filled my eyes and then flowed down my cheeks.

I heard footsteps coming down the stairs from the passage beyond. I willed myself to pretend that it was another demon trying to distract me so that I would let the fire burn my hand through completely. I refused to let the fire win, but the pain was nearly too much.

"What do you think you're doing?"

I sucked in a breath and pulled my hand free. I clenched it into a fist that hurt but not nearly as bad as it had in the fire. It took me several seconds to collect myself before I could meet Vicken's gaze.

"I'm practicing," I said. I forced my words not to tremble and betray how hard it had been on me.

His eyes widened at the look on my face. I realized I still had tears on my cheeks. Embarrassed, I turned away and used my sleeve to wipe them off.

"I'm not sure it's worth all that," he said, his voice careful.

I shook my head without looking at him. "Withstanding the pain is the only chance I have of saving your sister. I have to last longer than that."

"You're not the only one who can go against it," Vicken said, though he sounded unsure.

I made myself meet his gaze across the fire. "Who else is going to do it?" I asked. "We need Lyris and Brack to chant,

Dara and Alden can't do it, and I won't ask vampires to face their greatest fear."

"Why not?"

His words were quiet, contemplative. I realized his gaze was on the flame instead of me. The flickering light appeared eerie as it reflected in his yellow irises. Fear showed in their depths. Even though the flame was small, I knew his fears weren't to be downplayed.

When he reached his hand toward the flame, I said, "You don't have to do that."

He hesitated with his fingers an inch from the fire.

"You and I both want to save my sister," he said. "It's time I vamp up and do my part."

He shoved his hand into the flame.

His eyes widened at the all-too-real pain. I could see it on his face, the way he felt as if his flesh was melting. The fear became something more, as if losing his hand wasn't the only terror the fire could cause. His face twisted. I hurried to his side and put my hand on his arm. In the same way I had seen memories from the fox and two-headed cat, I pulled inward.

I saw the flame running up his arm and then encompassing his body. It spread quickly to the Academy, engulfing the school and all within in its grasp. The fire raced to a mansion on the edge of a great city and swallowed it as well until everything Vicken loved was devoured by green, writhing flames.

"I can't," Vicken said, pulling his hand free.

I let go and stared at him, my heart racing with the thoughts I had seen.

Vicken lowered his gaze and shook his head with abject disappointment on his face. "I can't do it," he said again. "I'm a coward."

"You're not a coward," I told him. "You tried even though I know how much you fear the fire."

"How can you know?" he asked. He spun to face me. "How can you even begin to understand?"

I realized he had no idea I had seen what he feared. I figured it wasn't the time to tell him. I looked back at the flame. "I'll keep practicing. I need to be ready for when we track down your sister."

Vicken's eyes narrowed. "We don't even have a lead, Finn. How are we possibly going to find her?" He shook his head. "You look like you're going to drop at any moment. Go get some sleep. Maybe you could actually think of how to find Amryn if you're not dead on your feet."

He left with those words ringing in my ears. I looked back at the candle, but I didn't have the strength to face it again that night. Taking the same care I did with putting it up, I set the flame back in its box and put it away. I reached for the box I had found in my mother's belongings, but then left it there with the thought that it would be much safer in the basement of the Academy than in my room.

I jogged slowly up the stairs, peeked through the spyholes beside the unicorn painting, then slipped out. Nobody was in the halls that late at night, or was it early in the morning? By the time I plugged my cellphone back in and fell into bed, I was sure the line between night and morning had definitely blurred.

"Goodnight," I said to the ghosts who stood around Alden's sleeping form. None of them answered me, but at least there were no green flames flickering in their gazes. I closed my eyes.

Vicken's voice repeated in my mind. 'Maybe you could actually think of how to find Amryn."

I closed my eyes with the hope that sleep was all I needed for that to happen.

Chapter Nine

I OPENED MY EYES and found myself standing. I blinked and realized I was in the cemetery again. The grass felt cold beneath my bare feet and the midnight breeze sent a chill across my arms. I glanced around at the sound of voices.

"Finn," someone whispered to my right.

I spotted Alden crouched behind one of the tombstones. He motioned for me to join him. At the urgent look on his face, I did so. It took me a moment to realize why it seemed strange to see him. He was alone; the ghosts that had become his constant companions had apparently given him a break for a moment.

"What are you doing here?" I asked him.

He motioned for me to keep my voice down and whispered, "I saw you sleepwalking, so I followed you here."

"Why are we being quiet?" I asked.

"Look," he said. He pointed over the tombstone.

I rose up on my knees and looked where he indicated.

Professor Briggs sat on the grass with his bad leg stretched in front of him. Perched on her tombstone, Mezania smiled down at him. But when she tipped her head, moonlight reflected off of tears that trailed down her cheeks. When Briggs looked up at her, matching tears showed on his face.

"I want to be a ghost with you," Briggs said, his voice thick with emotions. "You shouldn't have to be there without me."

"I want you to live," Mezania replied. She bent down and set a ghostly hand on his cheek. Her fingers brushed through instead of touching him. "I want you to live for both of us."

He shook his head as he held his cheek where her hand should have been. "I want to live where you live, even if that means we're both ghosts."

"You're needed here," Mezania said. "Your students need you."

"I can't do it without you," Briggs replied.

"But you must," Mezania told him, her voice breaking.

I felt horrible for overhearing such a personal conversation and knew that was why Alden was hiding. I slumped back down with my shoulders against the tombstone and gave him a sad look. The Grim nodded back with a sorrow-filled expression of his own.

I covered my ears to keep from overhearing more. My gaze drifted across the stones around us, then settled on one just over Alden's shoulder. A scent touched my nose and my blood ran cold. I rose to my feet.

"Finn, what are you doing?" Alden hissed.

He tried to pull me back down, but my attention stayed locked on the tombstone. I glanced back to verify what I already knew.

"What is this?" I asked aloud.

"What are you doing here?" Briggs demanded.

I heard him rise from his place near Mezania.

"He, uh, sleepwalked and I followed him," Alden said, fumbling over his words behind me.

"Stay away from Zanie," Briggs told him in a growl. "Neither of you should be here."

The professor grabbed my shoulder in a rough grip and tried to turn me around, but I refused to budge. I wish I had control of whatever werewolf strength made me so strong, but I didn't. At that moment, my feet were glued to the grass and I doubted the professor could have moved me even if he had been completely whole. He gave up and turned his attention to where I looked.

"What does that say?" I asked.

Scents of cinnamon and dew warred with the sulfurous cloying smell of demons. Among them, I could also smell the coppery scent of vampire.

"Every time I wake up here, I'm facing this direction," I said without taking my eyes off the tomb and the strange writing that marred the front of it. At first, I had taken them for scratches, but now it was obvious the marks were words. "I thought it was Mezania's headstone that drew me, but it's not."

Briggs studied it. "It says door."

"It does not," Mezania contradicted from beside him.

"You're better at reading Ilric than I," Briggs said. He stepped aside to give her space even though she could have gone through him if she wanted.

Out of the corner of my eye, I saw Mezania's ghostly form nod.

"That's because you never paid attention in class," she replied. She looked at the tomb. "The word means gateway. I can sense things trying to come through from the other side."

"What kind of things?" I asked.

She looked at me. "Something worse than demons."

A shiver ran down my spine. "We need to close the gateway."

"First," Briggs said in a level tone, "We need to open it and see if Amryn is in there." He glanced at Alden. "Summon the others."

"Right away," the Grim said. He ran from the cemetery.

Other marks showed on either side of the word.

"Are those fingerprints?" Mezania asked.

I nodded. "It looks like the way in. Maybe I should put my hands there."

"Maybe you should wait," Briggs suggested.

I shook my head. "I'd feel bad if Alden brought everyone here just to realize we don't know how to open it."

The professor was silent for a moment before he said, "You have a point. Try it."

I took a calming breath and put my hands on the tombstone. The stone was rough and cold beneath my fingertips. I don't know what I expected to happen, but given what the first ghost had said about the ghost of my heart and locking the door, I figured I would definitely be able to open it. But nothing happened.

I heard a sigh of frustration from Professor Briggs as if he, too, had expected at least something.

"Shouldn't it open?" Mezania said from Briggs' left.

"I thought so," I admitted with the same frustration in my voice.

The rest of the team arrived with an air of expectancy.

"You think she's down there?" Vicken asked without preamble.

"I do," I replied. "I can smell her."

Vicken rubbed his pale hands together. "Good. Let's bring her home."

"We, uh, can't," I said.

He stared at me. "Why not?"

"We can't open it," Briggs said. Inwardly I thanked him for sparing me the humiliation.

"Are those handprints?" Lyris asked.

"Yes," Mezania told her. "Try them."

"If Finn couldn't open it, I don't know how—"

"Let them try," Mezania said, cutting off Briggs' argument. Her voice softened and she said, "It can't hurt."

He nodded as though he would have done anything she asked of him.

Lyris took a calming breath the way I had done and put her hands to the tombstone. When nothing happened, she shot Dara a disappointed look over her shoulder. Dara followed with the same result. At Vicken's orders, the vampires tried, then Brack and Alden.

"Do it again," Vicken told me. "Aren't you supposed to be the one or something?"

I shook my head. "I'm not, but I'll try it again."

I did and felt ridiculously disappointed even though I had known it wouldn't work.

"My turn," Mercer said. He put his hands on the tombstone, covering the small handprints completely. When nothing happened, he shook his head. "Looks like we're stuck."

"We've got to get in there," Vicken fumed. He paced around the tombstone and studied the back as if hoping there were answers carved into the stone.

I sat on the grass and leaned against Mezania's headstone. She settled on top and hummed a quiet tune I didn't recognize.

"If it's a gateway," Lyris said. "Shouldn't we be able to enter it?"

"You would think," Dara replied wryly. "But you're also assuming we know what we're doing."

"We know what we're doing," Mercer said in his rough voice. But when the empath threw him a look, he shook his head. "Actually, we hardly know what we're doing when we think we do."

I ran the ghost's words over and over in my head. *The demons are restless and the fate of this school is in your hands. The ghost of your heart holds the key. Lock the door or all is lost.*

I had found the box in my mother's belongings. She was obviously the ghost of my heart even though I had mistakenly thought the riddle referred to Sebastian. But I didn't have a key. How could I lock the door without a key, or unlock it, for that matter?

I thought of the ghost's final words. He had called me Wolvenbracker, which Briggs had translated to wolf threat. A thought occurred to me. "Mezania, what does Wolvenbracker mean?"

She gave me a thoughtful look.

"I already told you. It means wolf threat," Briggs said from near the tombstone.

Mezania shook her head. "It means threat of the wolf. You're cutting corners like you always did," she told him with a twinkle in her eyes.

I looked from her to the professor. "Wait. What if we got this all wrong? What if what the ghost said wasn't for me at all?"

"What are you talking about?" Vicken asked irritably.

I ignored the vampire and rose. "Hear me out," I told the professor. "The ghost told me, 'The demons are restless and the fate of this school is in your hands. The ghost of your heart holds the key. Lock the door or all is lost.' And then he called me Wolvenbracker. But what if the message was for you, not me? I had your cloak across me in the infirmary because you let me borrow it when I was cold. You're the threat of the wolf because you killed my uncle Conrad." I realized by the reactions of my teammates around me that what I said wasn't common knowledge. I rushed on to say, "The ghost of your heart holds the key. I thought it was talking about my mom, but what if it meant—"

"Zanie," Briggs replied with awe in his voice.

"What?" Mezania said. "You meant I'm the one the ghost meant?"

I nodded. "You're the ghost of Briggs' heart for sure. If anyone is the key to opening that tomb, I think it's you."

She looked unsure. I could feel Briggs watching me as if I was crazy.

"But I can't touch the tombstone," she replied.

"It wouldn't hurt to try," Dara said.

I shot the empath a grateful look.

"Yeah," Lyris seconded. "What Finn says makes sense in a weird way."

"It's worth a try," Vicken admitted from behind the tombstone. "Why else would you be here?"

If his words hurt, the ghost didn't let it show.

"I-I guess it is," Mezania replied. "What do you think, Trace?"

He nodded. "I guess you could try."

She drifted closer to the tombstone. Briggs kept protectively close to her side. As if worried that it would hurt, Mezania held out her hands and closed her eyes. Just when I was worried that her hands would go through the stone, they stopped on the surface as if they were as solid as mine.

Mezania's eyes flew open and she exclaimed when the fingermarks lit up in an eerie shade of green.

"It worked," Alden breathed.

The tombstone slid backwards to reveal a set of cement stairs leading beneath where the coffin should have been. Everyone stared into the dark hole.

"Are you sure we should go in there?" Lyris asked. Worry showed in her gaze as she looked down the dark stairway.

"We have to," Vicken and I said at the same time.

Mercer gave a noncommittal grunt and looked at me. "I know why Fangs here wants to go, so why you?"

I realized I hadn't told them about the box yet. "I found something," I began.

"Why do I have the feeling this is going to be a long story?" Vicken interrupted. "Have you forgotten about my sister?"

"It might help us find her, or at least stop him," I replied.

"Him who?" Briggs asked.

"Chutka the Shambler," I said.

"Where did you hear that name?" Mercer demanded.

"Isn't that the name the demon said before he died?" Lyris asked, her gaze worried.

"I think he's at the bottom of this," I told them. "Dara and I found a demon sigil in the clubhouse after you guys left."

Dara nodded in affirmation.

I could feel everyone's gazes when I continued with, "I remembered seeing the same sigil on a box with my mom's stuff, so I went home—"

"You left the Academy without permission?" Professor Briggs cut in. "That was dangerous. You could have been caught by the Maes or worse. Someone could have seen you phase."

I didn't want to point out the truth of his statements. Instead, I rushed on with, "I'm sorry. I won't do it again. But I found the box."

"What was inside?" Vicken asked with only a hint of interest.

"Another box."

"Of course," the vampire replied with a sigh.

"I can't open it, but the first box was marked with the same sigil. I think that's the key we need to find."

"I thought Mezania was the key," Jean said with confusion in his voice.

"She was, but now we need another key," I said.

Vicken threw up his hands in disgust. "Whatever. Let's just get in the hole and find my sister. If you happen to find a key, great."

Mercer grunted. "If the key to Finn's box is down there, we could be that much closer to stopping this ghost and demon infestation."

The same thought had crossed my mind.

"I need to go down there. You guys can stay," I told them.

Everyone was quiet for a moment before Dara said, "As if we'd let you have all the adventures on your own."

Strained laughter followed and I smiled because I really didn't think they would let me go alone. To be honest, I felt much better at the thought of them having my back.

"Looks, um, inviting," Mezania said.

"You should stay up here," Briggs told her. He eyed Alden and said gruffly, "And you need to come with us."

"Of course," Alden replied.

I went first because I could see in the dark. Alden followed close behind me. He clicked on the flashlight he had used to follow me to the cemetery and said in a whisper, "I understand his problem with me, but he could handle it a bit better."

I glanced back to see Vicken, Dara, and then Professor Briggs follow us down with the others close behind. The uncertainty on the faces of my friends reminded me that we had no idea where we were going. I continued down the steep stairway.

"You heard him talking to Mezania. I think he's afraid of losing what time they have left together, and he just doesn't know how to face life without her again."

Alden let out a breath behind me. "Grims don't have a choice, you know?"

I looked back at him. "What do you mean?"

"With the people they are told to take. They don't have a choice." His voice was quieter when he said, "My parents say it's not easy, but we have to be professional and not get involved."

I hadn't really thought about the work of a Grim from the Grim's point of view. "It's got to be hard knowing what you're going to do after the Academy," I told him.

He was quiet a moment, then he gave a little chuckle and said, "I suppose not as hard as not knowing what you are until your body decides to let you in on the secret that you're a werewolf and now everyone's afraid of you."

That brought an answering chuckle from me. "That was definitely a surprise."

"Are you guys laughing down there?" Vicken demanded.

I shot Alden a look. He gave me a wide-eyed one back and we continued down in silence. I realized after the sound of footsteps became the only thing I could hear that both Alden and I had been talking to keep the tension at bay. Walking further down than I imagined the Academy basement to be put me on edge. I swore I heard something further on and paused, but when nothing came up the stairs, I continued on.

"What if these stairs never stop?" Brack asked. His deep voice echoed along the tunnel.

"Then we'll just go back," Lyris reassured him.

"As long as he doesn't panic and trap us all in here," Dara muttered.

"You do say the most pleasant things," Vicken told her.

"Quiet, everyone," Briggs told them. "Give Finn a chance to hear danger coming if he can."

"Nothing's coming," Vicken said. "Nothing but this never-ending staircase."

Then it changed. Instead of walking downward, I had the distinct impression we were walking back up even though we kept moving down. It was the strangest sensation. I felt a tickling in my stomach and my head felt lighter.

"Anyone else disoriented?" Mercer asked from the back of the group.

"Yeah, I thought I was going crazy," Jean said.

"Me, too," Lorne agreed. "I feel like I'm upside-down or something."

We drew near to a threshold. The tunnel was lit from beyond the stairway. Relief filled me at the lessening of darkness. The relief faded when I reached the threshold and looked beyond.

"What in the world?" Alden said from behind me.

"I don't understand it," I replied.

We stood on the ceiling of the Academy corridor looking up to look down. It made no sense. Students rushed underneath as if in a hurry. I could just see the clock through the door to the cafeteria. Apparently breakfast had just started. I wondered if we had truly been climbing down the stairs for that long.

"What is it?" Vicken asked. "I want to see."

He shoved everyone forward. I wavered on the edge of the threshold, afraid of falling into the Academy.

"Hold on," I said. "Just—"

Vicken pushed again and I fell inside. Alden grabbed my sleeve, but he couldn't stop me. Instead of falling down, well, up, I landed on my knees on the ceiling. My heart thundered in my chest as I looked up at the students who walked through the hall above me as if they weren't upside down at all.

"That's trippy," Dara said as Alden gingerly followed me inside.

"Where are we?" Vicken asked. His yellow eyes were wide as he looked up at the students who were oblivious of our presence. Ghosts wandered along the ceiling and floor, walking through us as though they didn't see us either.

"We're in the Otherworld," Professor Briggs said as he followed the rest of our team onto the ceiling.

"Have you been here before?" Lyris asked him.

The professor shook his head. "No, but I've read about it."

He watched Mercer climb over the threshold. The sweeper stared around him. "Me, too. But I never thought I'd see it with my own eyes."

"What are those?"

I followed Alden's finger to a dark shadow that trailed behind one of the students. It wasn't one of the many ghosts that wandered between them. A chill ran down my spine. I followed the student from the ceiling until I crossed the threshold to the cafeteria. The chill turned into a cold brick in my stomach at the sight of other shadows hovering behind students, watching as they ate, following their conversations, and mimicking their gestures.

"They're demons," Mercer said.

One of the shadows glanced up and I saw the green fire in its eyes.

"There's so many of them," Dara said in a voice just above a whisper.

"What are they doing?" Brack asked.

"Imitating," Briggs said. "Preparing to take over."

A dark figure entered the cafeteria without following a student. My heart slowed as the figure solidified. He was huge with black shadow armor and a helmet that showed the glow of green demon eyes within. A hole in his helmet revealed a mouth that was filled with pointed teeth when he spoke words I couldn't understand. The students we saw didn't appear to hear him, but the demons listened with rapt attention.

"Is that a knight?" Lorne asked.

"The Demon Knight," Alden said.

"What did you say?" Mercer asked.

Alden's eyes widened and he looked at me. "Finn said to find out information about Chutka the Shambler after the demon said it in the corridor. So I looked." He nodded toward the demon below. "According to the book I found, that's the Demon Knight, Chutka's first subordinate. He has two more, the—"

"The Wiccan Enforcer and the Darkest Warlock," Mercer finished. He was watching Alden with a disapproving look. "You were reading forbidden books."

"I figured they weren't forbidden to us if we needed to know," Alden replied with only a hint of nervousness in his words.

"So the Demon Knight is teaching them how to imitate students?" Lyris asked. "What then?"

"Think about it," Dara told her. "If they can take over the students and then go home to their families, demons will be all over the country."

"We've got to stop it," I said.

"But what if—"

Alden dropped his flashlight. Instead of it landing at our feet like I expected, the light turned end on end as it fell upward and then hit the Demon Knight on the shoulder.

Chapter Ten

EVERYONE GASPED WHEN THE Demon Knight looked up at us. The glowing green orbs that made up his eyes narrowed. He put his hands together and a ball of red fire appeared between them.

"Run!" Briggs shouted.

The Knight threw the fireball at us. I shoved my teammates ahead of me toward the door, but there was no way we would make it in time. I thought of Professor Briggs' words about how dangerous demon fire was to any mythic; I could only imagine that the red fire from the Demon Knight was even worse. If the vampires went up in flames and the witch and warlock were injured like Briggs, the team didn't have a chance. The Alpha in me surged. I refused to see any of my teammates fall at the hands of the Knight.

Dara and Lyris ran through the door. Alden tripped. Briggs pulled him upright and shoved the student in front of him. There was no way they would make it. I turned and stood in the way of the fireball.

"Finn!" Mercer shouted from the other side of the door with more emotion in his voice than he had ever shown on his face.

"No!" Dara exclaimed.

I didn't dare look back to see if they had made it through. I couldn't let the fireball get past me. I gritted my teeth and held up my hands even though I knew they couldn't protect me from the huge writhing mass of red flames.

Sparrow lifted her head from my wrist. She looked back at me, her green eyes bright. Then, before I could stop her, the little dragon launched herself off my hand toward the fireball. She spread her wings just before it hit. The red fireball engulfed her completely and then vanished. To my horror, the sylph dragon's wings faltered, her eyes closed, and she fell lifelessly toward the Demon Knight below.

"No!" I shouted. I jumped and grabbed her body from the air. When my feet hit the ground, I met the eyes of the Demon Knight.

He glared at me as he formed another fireball in his hands.

"You don't belong here," he said.

The growl of his voice tore through me like a rabid dog. I sucked in a breath at the chill that shook my soul.

The Demon Knight tipped his head. "You'd better run."

I realized it was a game for him. He was toying with us and Sparrow had just taken the fall for it. I let out a growl and was looking for some way to attack him when a voice barked from the doorway.

"Finn, get out of there!"

129

The command in Briggs' voice tore me from the stupidity of my actions. I ran for the door. I glanced back in time to see another fireball hurling our way. I dove across the threshold and heard the fire hit the wall next to where I had been.

The rest of my team was already running up the stairs. I hurried after Briggs who pushed himself mercilessly despite the pain it must have caused to his damaged leg. About halfway up, his steps faltered. I ducked under his arm and we made our way up as fast as we could.

"Hurry," a voice said beside me.

"They're coming," another whispered.

I looked to my left to see two ghosts rushing alongside us. Glancing around, I saw other glowing figures urging us back up the steps. There was fear on their faces; my heart tightened when I realized their fear was for us.

Below, the sound of claws on stone sounded. I could see green eyes glowing in the darkness.

"We've got to hurry," I told the professor.

"I know," he replied tightly. "Go on ahead."

I shook my head. "You're going to make it."

Together, we climbed more stairs than I could count. The square of moonlight above that made up the doorway felt further and further away, but we didn't give up. The sounds of the claws drew closer, spurring us on. I could hear Lyris, Dara, and the others calling our names. Finally, we burst through the door and sprawled on the grass.

"Close it!" Mercer commanded.

Out of the corner of my eye, I saw Mezania put her hands to the tombstone again. It slid shut, muting the angry howls of the demons beneath.

"Brack, make sure it's shut tight," Professor Briggs said.

The huge warlock nodded. "It's done."

I climbed to my feet despite the way my knees shook.

"Where are you going?" Mercer demanded.

"I need to find Professor Seedly so he can help Sparrow," I said. Tears burned in my eyes, but I refused to let them fall. The little dragon's body felt so fragile in my hand. I didn't know how badly the fire had hurt her, but I had to get help right away. I could feel the call of the moonlight, but ignored it. I took another step toward the Academy.

"It's too late, Finn-wolf."

My heart slowed at Lyris' words. I looked back at her, wondering what she meant. I didn't have time to wait around. I had to help Sparrow. I had to—

A tiny spirit sat on Mezania's tombstone. The ghost knelt and stroked the little dragon with her fingers. Sparrow tipped her head to the side and closed her eyes the way she did when she enjoyed being petted.

"No," I whispered. The need to phase surged harder. I shoved it away.

Tears trickled down Lyris' face when she looked at me. "I'm so sorry, Finn."

I shook my head. "No. It can't be."

I opened my hand. Sparrow's little body didn't move. I dropped to my knees and willed her head to lift and her wings to open.

"Come on, Sparrow, look at me." My voice broke.

I ran a finger gently down her back. When I took it away, red soot covered my skin. Pain knotted in my stomach at ignoring the phase. I gritted my teeth.

"Finn," Briggs said, his voice soft.

I shook my head. "She didn't deserve to die." I forced myself to look at the little creature on the tombstone. She tipped her head at Mezania the way she did to me when I spoke to her.

"C-can she see me?" I asked the ghost.

131

Mezania shook her head. The tears on her cheeks caught in the moonlight. "She's on her way beyond," the ghost said.

My breath caught in my throat. "T-take good care of her, will you?" I asked.

Mezania nodded. "I will. I promise."

I doubled over with the pain of denying the phase and set my forehead on the cool grass.

"Finn, are you alright?" Vicken asked.

I shook my head.

Dara set a hand on my shoulder. I felt her pull and heard the accompanying intake of her breath at my pain.

"He needs to phase," she told the team. "Give him space." She knelt next to me. "Can I take Sparrow?"

I shook my head again and set the body gently on the grass. "I'll take care of her," I said. My voice cracked with the knowledge that I hadn't taken care of her at all. If it wasn't for me, she would still be alive, chasing flies and blowing little blue mint-scented flames.

A sob tore through me and the phase took over. I felt my shirt rip but I didn't care. I knew my teammates watched me, but couldn't find the strength to be embarrassed. The phase hurt because I fought it and I used the pain to chase away any other thought. Pain to fight pain was a useless venture, but I clung to it to block out thoughts of how I had failed Sparrow when she saved me instead of the other way around.

I stood in wolf form with my head hung low and my chest heaving at the exertion of changing form.

"F-Finn, are you alright?" Dara asked.

I padded slowly to Mezania's tomb and began to dig. It was a small hole. The thought that it was still huge for her made my heart ache. I didn't care that digging through the cold ground hurt my damaged paw. When I picked up Sparrow's body carefully in my mouth and set it in the hole, I heard crying but didn't look up to see who it was. I used my nose to push the dirt back the best that I could. My teammates knelt around me and helped with the dirt as well, patting it down better than I was able.

I stepped back and found myself at eye level with the little dragon on Mezania's tombstone. She met my gaze, her green eyes bright and her black and purple tail flicking from side to side. On impulse, I lowered my head so that my chin rested on the cold stone. Sparrow nuzzled my nose. For the briefest instant, I could feel it. It was almost as if the moonlight granted us that brief moment in which to say goodbye. I wished I could cry as a wolf. Tears would have been much easier to bear than the way my heart broke in my chest. When I opened my eyes, the little dragon had moved to Mezania's hand. She curled around the ghost's wrist and closed her eyes.

I couldn't take it anymore. I turned away and began to run.

"Finn, wait!" Dara called.

I ducked my head and ran faster, leaping logs and mountain streams until I had left the cemetery far behind. Sparrow was gone. The thought pounded over and over in my mind. I had let her down. I had failed to protect her. I had placed her in the path of danger and done nothing when she sacrificed herself to save me.

She had acted so quickly I didn't know what to do. In the back of my mind, I thought she would be impervious to the fire like she had been when the demon attacked. Seeing her engulfed by the red flame was devastating, and when I caught her in my hand, I had known she was gone despite the denial that flooded my mind.

Footsteps sounded behind me. I swerved to the right, intent on losing whoever tried to follow. To my shock, a massive force slammed into me and sent me rolling. I stopped against a tree and shook my head, dazed.

"Where are you going?" Vicken demanded.

He climbed to his feet and brushed off his grass-stained pants. Even in the moonlight, I could tell they were ruined.

I growled at him.

Vicken glared at me. "You think you can just run off and leave everyone like that? You think you're the only one who's sad that Sparrow's dead?"

My ear twitched at the catch in his voice when he said the dragon's name. I turned away from him.

"Don't you dare do that," the vampire said.

He grabbed my shoulder.

I turned on him with a snarl.

"Seriously?" he replied. "That's how it's going to be?"

He picked me up so fast I could barely believe it. I rolled my shoulders and pushed off of him before he could get a good grip. The moment my paws hit the ground, he had me in a bearhug. I ducked my head and pushed away from him at the same time. He let out an oomph at the force of my paws in his stomach, but he scrambled to grab me again.

I told myself not to hurt him. Instincts whispered at the back of my mind that we were playing a very dangerous game. Somewhere in our history, vampires and werewolves had been mortal enemies. Since there hadn't been a werewolf around since my mother left the Academy twenty-five years ago, that hostility had faded until I attended the Academy. The venom I had seen in Don Ruvine's eyes wasn't new to me. Though Vicken and I walked a very fine line between enemy and teammate, things could get bad quicker than I could stop it if I wasn't careful.

His hands gripped the fur of my back so hard it hurt. I twisted like a cat and lunged at his face. My teeth snapped shut inches from his forehead. Caught by surprise, he let me go and I hit the ground. I was about to leap at him again when a scent caught my nose. I turned, searching for the source.

134

"Giving up so easily?" Vicken taunted. "Afraid you'll be beaten by a vampire?"

I ignored him and sniffed the air. The cloying sulfurous scent was thicker beyond the bushes.

"What, are you following a rabbit now?" Vicken asked with disgust in his voice. "You really are an animal, aren't you?"

I wished I could shut him up. Instead, I paced toward the scent.

"If you catch a rabbit, you better be prepared to share. I haven't had blood in a while and it would be nice to have something fresh," the vampire muttered as he followed me through the bushes.

I lowered my head in order to keep track of the scent and ran faster. A glance over my shoulder showed Vicken keeping up easily. Apparently a vampire's strength also gave them plenty of stamina for midnight jaunts through the forest.

We reached a clearing near a rocky mountain ledge and I slowed, testing the air. The scent had disappeared. I turned in a circle, checking for where I had lost it.

"Nothing?" Vicken said. "We go this far and for what?" He kicked a rock in disgust. It bounced over the edge of the cliff and down the steep side.

A sound caught my ear and I spun, facing the direction we had come.

"What are you—"

I gave a low growl and he fell silent. Steps sounded again. They were huge. I ran through the list of mythical creatures I knew, which wasn't many. The bushes in front of me swayed from side to side. An unfamiliar musk filled the air along with the sulfurous scent.

I let out a growl and took a step back. Vicken backed up as well.

"Finn, what is that?" he whispered.

I shook my head with my gaze locked on the bushes. They were thick and thorny, towering far above my head in this older part of the forest. With the ledge at our back and the mountain rising sharply to the side, the path around the bushes remained our only route back to the Academy.

The Alpha side of me balked at cowering from a threat I didn't know. My fur rose as the beast drew closer. I took a step forward and growled.

"Is that smart?" Vicken asked. "It could just wander away and—"

The biggest bear I had ever seen crashed through the bushes with a snarl of rage. It swung its head from side to side, glaring at me with beady eyes that glowed with green fire.

Vicken and I both scrambled back to the edge of the cliff.

"Do you see its eyes?" Vicken asked, his voice tight with fear.

I snorted to let him know I had.

"When did demons start possessing animals?" he demanded.

The bear shuffled its feet. Black claws large enough to gut me tore into the forest loam. The bear let out a bellow loud enough to awaken everyone at the Academy. Hatred flickered in its glowing eyes, revealing the demon that had taken over where the animal should have been. I knew when I looked into its gaze that the creature had been sent to kill us.

"Run to the right," Vicken said quietly.

I glanced back at him.

He nodded toward the path by the bushes. "I'll distract it. Run to the path and get out of here." He met my gaze. "Just promise you'll save Amryn. I think you're the only one who can."

It took me a moment to realize the vampire was about to sacrifice himself to save me. I couldn't help staring.

"On the count of three," Vicken continued, oblivious of my shock. His chest rose and fell in fear of what he was about to do, but he kept his eyes on the bear. He stooped and picked up a rock. "One, two...."

The bear charged before he could reach three. Vicken dove to the left as I darted to the right. The animal followed the vampire. Vicken threw his rock. It hit the bear hard on the snout. The beast rose up on its hind legs with a roar and knocked the vampire down with a huge paw. Before Vicken could get back up, the bear stepped on him. Its claws tore into his chest.

"Run!" Vicken gasped out.

A normal person with proper sensibilities might have run away at the sight of a demon-possessed bear, but I was neither normal nor had proper sensibilities. I was an Alpha werewolf with apparently great expertise at getting into trouble. I didn't know how to walk away.

I gathered my legs beneath me and leaped onto the bear's back. The beast rose up again in an attempt to throw me off, but I bit its shoulder and refused to let go for fear that if it landed back down, it would do so on top of Vicken.

"Idiot!" I heard Vicken say before the bear turned and slammed me into the boulders that made up the side of the mountain.

Winded, I lost my grip and fell when the bear backed away. It turned and was about to step on me when it let out a roar and lumbered in the other direction. I pushed myself up using the boulders in time to see Vicken heft another rock the size of my head.

"That's right, demon. Come pick on someone with a little more intelligence."

He shot me a look. I rolled my eyes and limped closer. I was afraid that the bear would charge the vampire and take him over the edge. The thought gave me an idea. I crept quietly around its left side as it advanced on Vicken. He lifted the rock menacingly.

"You really want this?" the vampire asked. "I'm more than happy to give it to you."

Before he could throw it, I darted in and nipped the bear's back leg. The creature spun with a bellow. I danced back fast enough to avoid a sweep of its claws and ran around to its other side.

"What are you doing?" Vicken demanded.

I nipped at the bear again. It spun once more, its eyes glowing with vile hatred.

This time when I ran around it, I did so closer to the edge so that when I stopped, the cliff was only about a foot behind me.

"Finn," Vicken warned.

The bear swung its massive head toward him. I growled and its attention locked back on me.

"Finn, the ledge," Vicken said.

I ran around the bear's side, intent on driving it backwards. My burned paw slipped on a rock and I stumbled. The creature pinned me to the ground with a heavy paw. Its head lowered. I felt the wash of its putrid breath and wondered what kind of disease I could catch from a demon-possessed bear. It opened its mouth to bite me. Before it could close its jaws, a rock smashed into its face.

The bear rose up again with a roar. It swiped at Vicken, but the vampire dodged with superhuman speed. I saw my chance. Before the beast could lower back down, I sprang at its chest. The bear stumbled backwards with the force of the attack. I bit at its throat. The bear clawed at me in an attempt to tear me free, but I stubbornly held on. I felt it take one step back and then another. I put my paws against it, ready to spring free when it fell.

To my dismay, the bear wrapped me in a bone-crushing hug, trapping me against it. I struggled to break free, but it wouldn't let go. It took another step backwards as it tried to squeeze the life from me. I felt one hind paw slip and then the other. My heart leaped in my throat at the feeling of plummeting through the air. I closed my eyes and then yelped.

Hands gripped my tail, tearing me from the bear's grasp when it fell off the ledge. Vicken pulled me unceremoniously back up as I stared at the bear rolling down the side of the cliff. It stopped close to the bottom and rose shakily to its feet. It looked up at us. I couldn't tell from that distance if the green fire was gone from its gaze, but whatever fight had filled it had apparently left because the bear turned away and lumbered in the opposite direction from where we stood.

"Well that was exciting," Vicken said dryly. He put his hand to his chest and pulled it away to show dark blood on his pale palm. He rubbed his hand on his pant leg. "Remind me to follow you into the forest less often."

I gave a snort and willed my racing heart to slow. Vicken bent over with his hands on his knees, showing the first sign of exhaustion I had ever seen from the vampire.

"That was interesting," he noted as he drew in a breath. "Why do you think—"

A scream caught my ear. I rose with my attention on the path.

"What is it?" Vicken asked, straightening.

I barked and then took off running.

"Again with the running," Vicken called. "Haven't you learned that it doesn't turn out well?"

Chapter Eleven

MORE SCREAMS FILLED THE air before we reached the cemetery. When we arrived at the clearing, I skidded to a stop at the sight of my team backed against a set of trees. Two mountain lions paced back and forth in front of them.

"More demon-possessed animals?" Vicken said, coming to a halt beside me.

Both mountain lions looked back at us. The green fire in their eyes was unmistakable.

"Vicken, Finn, be careful!" Lorne warned.

A copper scent lay heavy in the air. I dared a glance at my team and found the source. Mercer was leaning against a tree with his hands clutching his stomach. The shirt he held as a bandage was covered in blood. A glance to the left showed Brack with claw marks down his bare chest.

"They're in trouble," Vicken said under his breath.

I growled. Both cougars turned completely around.

"Now we're in trouble," the vampire said with a touch of irony.

I let out another growl and took a step back. Both mountain lions advanced.

"Run for the school," Vicken told our team. He retreated with me, keeping his gaze on the cougars.

I looked up just long enough to see Lorne and Jean helping Mercer to his feet while Lyris and Dara assisted Brack. Professor Briggs kept between the team and the threat of the mountain lions as the students and professors retreated toward the Academy.

One of the cougars looked back at the group. Vicken picked up a stick and threw it. It hit the big cat on the rump with painful accuracy. The mountain lion spun back to face him and hissed. They both advanced toward us with deadly grace.

"Now we've got their attention, but I don't think your little stunt with the bear is going to help us," Vicken said as we both backed up. "I doubt we can make it to the ridge before they take us down. I hope you have a different plan."

I was glad I was in wolf form so I didn't have to admit that my plan hadn't gone beyond getting the creatures' attention to distract them from our team. I growled again to ensure that they would follow, then took off running.

"Running again?" Vicken said when he caught up to me. "Is this some sort of wolf thing?"

Ironically, it was the only wolf thing I was good at, or the only one I knew, for that matter. I was grateful that at least with Vicken's vampire strength, he could keep up with me. But the sound of the cougars behind us told me that they were catching up very quickly. If we didn't find an escape soon, we were going to have to fight them, and after experiencing the demon-possessed strength of the bear, I was anxious to avoid another encounter.

The sound of a river caught my ear. I veered to the right and heard Vicken follow. The short gasps of the vampire's breaths told me that his strength was waning. Given all we had confronted since I awoke in the cemetery, I was amazed we were both still running. My own breath came in short spurts. Both of us were surviving on sheer adrenaline.

My path took us to a river about twenty feet across. The rush of the water around boulders as it swept above the sides of the riverbed told of rain further up in the mountain. Logs and forest debris were pulled past. Vicken and I stopped and turned to face the demon-possessed animals. I second-guessed my plan as I placed myself between the vampire and the cougars. I tried to tell myself that we were going to be fine, but the huge cats bore down on us with the intent to kill bright in their flaming eyes.

I glanced at the water.

"I'm not doing what you seem to be thinking about doing," Vicken said. He eyed the hunting cats warily.

The creatures advanced, snarling and spitting their rage at our elusiveness.

I took a step toward the river. As uninviting as it looked, it was our only hope.

"Don't even think about it," Vicken said.

I backed up another step, forcing him to do the same. The cougars faced us down, their green eyes roiling in hatred. I didn't relish the thought of their claws in my hide. In wolf form or human, they were bound to hurt very badly. I took another step.

"Has anyone ever told you you're crazy?" Vicken asked when his next step took him into the shallow water that lapped above the bank.

I waded into the water beside him. There was a small lip, and then the water ran deep enough that I couldn't see the bottom through the rush. The feeling of the cold water against my paws wasn't a welcome one, but we were out of options. I only hoped we had distracted the cougars long enough for our team to reach the Academy.

A glance at Vicken showed his reluctance to enter the river. I looked back in time to see the mountain lions crouched as one and prepare to spring. The moment their huge paws left the ground, I lunged back at Vicken, propelling us both into the icy water.

Yowls of surprise filled the air as the cougars landed in the river as well. Their splashing and wailing was the last thing I heard before the tangled branches of a stump took me under.

I was back in the car. This time it was completely submerged. Sebastian lolled lifelessly next to me. I could hear Drake's muted struggles in the back seat, but couldn't get my seatbelt off to save him. I fought as hard as I could. I remembered yanking on the belt to free myself, but it wouldn't work this time. The belt was rough and scratchy instead of smooth and cloth. It wouldn't yield to my struggles.

My last breath left in a cloud of bubbles. I couldn't see Sebastian anymore. The water was dark and cold; my limbs ached with the chill that permeated deeper than anything I had ever experienced. I fought to keep my mouth closed. The knowledge that a breath of water would be my last made me battle the need to breathe. Darkness filled my vision and a humming sound rose in my ears. I didn't want to die underwater. The thought sounded over and over in my mind. It was a horrible way to die. I owed it to Drake to live and see that he didn't suffer the same death as Sebastian. But I couldn't free myself in order to save him.

Hands grabbed my right arm. I paused in confusion, wondering who was trying to help me when it was supposed to be my job to save the others, a job I had already failed once.

The hands pulled and pain exploded in my burned hand. I gulped in despite my resolve and choked on the water. The hands wouldn't let go; instead, they pulled harder. The rough seatbelt scraped against my chest, and then I was free.

When my head broke the surface, I tried to breathe, but the water that clogged my lungs refused to let me. I was pulled to the edge of a bank and shoved up.

"Breathe!" Vicken shouted as he pulled himself up beside me. "Come on, Finn. Take a breath!"

With my blurry vision I saw his head block out the moonlight.

Fear was bright in the vampire's eyes as he shouted again, "Come on, Finn! Don't you dare give up now!"

His voice rang tinny and muted to my ears. My head lolled to the side despite my efforts to focus.

Vicken brought both hands up in a club and slammed them down on my chest. I doubled over in pain and the water shot from my mouth. I gasped in a huge breath and coughed, sucking in another painful gulp of air.

"That's it," Vicken said. He sat back with one hand on his chest and the other on my shoulder. "Keep breathing. Take your time. We're safe."

I focused on breathing until it stopped hurting so badly. It took me some time to realize that I was in my human form again. I must have changed when we hit the water. I knew the fact that I was naked would be far more horrific once I convinced my body I was no longer drowning. Fortunately, vampires got cold easily due to their low blood levels and tended to dress in lots of layers. The wet trench coat Vicken tossed over was long enough to cover most of me. I pulled it on gingerly.

"Take it easy," Vicken said. "I'm pretty sure you almost died."

"Do you see Alden...close by?" I asked, breaking to cough up more water.

A pained smile touched the vampire's lips. "No. Why? Do you think he needs more ghosts to haunt him?"

I nodded. "Definitely." I sucked in a breath and was glad when it didn't hurt as badly. "It adds a bit of uniqueness to his character, don't you think?"

"As if a Grim needs more uniqueness," Vicken replied. He chuckled and then grabbed his chest.

In the light of dawn, I could make out the four claws marks from the bear stepping on him. Blood that was nearly black streaked his dirty shirt.

"You need to get those bandaged," I told him.

He shook his head wearily. "I don't think I'm going anywhere."

"What are you talking about?" I asked. "We need to get back to the Academy. Dr. Six will patch you up in no time."

Vicken let out a sigh and shook his head again. "You remember when I told you that I haven't had blood in a while? It's because I've been so worried about Amryn that I haven't been eating."

"You what?" I sat up with my instincts tingling. "How long has it been since you've eaten?"

Vicken studied the ground by my bare foot. "I can't remember," he admitted.

His words slurred slightly. I remembered Professor Tripe saying that vampires should drink fresh blood at least every two days under normal circumstances. Given the demon bear, running for our lives seemingly every two seconds, and all of the stress of the last few days with the ghosts and

145

demons and his sister's disappearance combined with his mother being taken by the Maes, these definitely weren't normal circumstances.

I had thought that the blood staining his shirt was dark due to dirt from the river, but a closer look showed that it came from the wounds that way. It was the last vestiges of what was left after his body used what it could of the remaining blood. I could hear the sluggish beating of his heart as it did what it could. He was dying.

"Vicken, you need blood," I said.

He gave me a tired half-smile. "I'm wishing you had...caught that rabbit."

I slid the sleeve of the trench coat up. "Drink."

Vicken looked from my proffered wrist to my face. "What?" Incomprehension made his yellow eyes dull.

"Drink," I told him. "You just pulled me from the river. I owe you my life and I'm not about to see you die when I can do something about it. Drink what you need."

He pushed himself away from me. "You-you don't know what you're asking."

I nodded. "Yes, I do. If you don't drink fresh blood, you'll die. I could hunt for some animal, but between the two of us, I've never killed anything and I don't even know the first thing about hunting. This is your best option." I held out my hand again. "Take it."

Vicken watched me closely. I studied him, noting that he was swaying slightly from side to side while he sat there. His skin was far paler than it should have been and the brightness of his yellow eyes had lessened to a dull mustard color. He was fading quickly.

"You'll get sick."

I nodded. "I know what I'm getting into."

Professor Tripe had also taught that when a vampire bites his victim, willing or not, the vampire passes a pathogen into

146

the victim's bloodstream that can cause lethargy, dizziness, and sometimes even put the victim into a coma. He said that this was so the victim would be readily available if the vampire was unable to drink his or her fill, and something about this being an evolutionary trait that helped vampires survive in hiding during the massacres.

Vicken doubled over with both hands to his chest. I heard his heart give a loud thump, followed by several shallow ones. When Vicken straightened again, the blood that covered his hands was a sticky black color.

"I'm not giving you a choice," I told him. I held the coat closed as I leaned toward him. "Drink, now, or we're both dead out here."

"Why's that?" the vampire asked, his gaze on the wrist I held in front of him.

The fact that it was the wrist Sparrow usually slept around made my heart hurt. I welcomed the bite of fangs to dull that kind of pain.

"Because I'm not leaving you. Those demon cougars will probably find us if we stay here and neither of us is in any shape to fight them," I said honestly.

I shoved my arm in his face. Just when I thought I would have to come up with yet another ironic argument as to why he should drink my blood, Vicken opened his mouth and bit my wrist.

It hurt. I hadn't actually thought of the pain of having fangs sink through my skin. It felt like the time I had cut myself on a rusty bar while skateboarding and had to get stitches. The numbing injections were the worse part because the doctor put them inside the wound. I remembered telling Julianne I would rather have had the stitches without being numb than go through that again.

Having my blood drank by Vicken felt like what I imagined having the stitches without being numb would feel.

Each gulp he drew in made my arm go even colder. While the vampire's drinking fangs had elongated in order to draw the blood, his other teeth had also sharpened so that they cut into my arm on either side as well. I was sure Professor Tripe would say that it was so the victim couldn't get away while the vampire drank his fill. I wondered if the professor would give himself up as a willing candidate in order to more correctly describe the effects of this type of blood donation.

The chill ran up my arm and along my chest. My head began to swim with strange thoughts. I wondered if I would have turned into a fish if I had stayed beneath the water long enough. I thought that if I had been a dragon, I could have carried the car to safety after it fell off the bridge. I thought of Dara's lips on mine in a kiss that felt so far away and yet so important it lingered in the back of my mind even when I was on the verge of passing out.

I was going to pass out. The realization made me open my eyes. I had lost too much blood. Instincts pressed urgently at the back of my mind. If I let Vicken continue to drink, I would die.

"V-Vicken, you need to s-stop," I said. My teeth chattered when I spoke. I had no idea whether it was from the chill of the night air against the wet coat I wore or the weakness I felt at the loss of blood.

Vicken continued to drink with his eyes closed and his hands on either side of my arm to hold it in place.

I cleared my burning throat and tried again. "V-Vicken. S-stop drinking."

He acted as if he couldn't hear me. Perhaps he was also animal in a way that made him fight for survival above all else. I knew the feeling when I had fought the bear in wolf form. No matter how hard I fought, survival was at the foremost of my instincts. Maybe we weren't so different.

If I couldn't reason with him in words, I had another route. I took a breath and let my instincts take over. The growl that rumbled from my chest didn't sound as though it came from a human. Even the cougars would have thought twice about messing with me if they heard the sound. I was proud and a little bit frightened at the fact that I had made it.

Vicken's head jerked up. He looked at me with wide eyes while blood, my blood, dripped down his chin. He stared as if he didn't recognize me.

"You've had enough," I said firmly.

He blinked and understanding surfaced in his gaze. He looked down at my arm and then back at my face.

"You let me drink your blood."

His statement was filled with shock. I realized that with the dullness of his eyes before and the way his speech slurred, he hadn't even been aware enough of what was going on to know what he did. But the bright yellow had returned to his irises and the pallor of his cheeks had lessened. He sat back, his eyes wide as he looked down at my bloody wrist.

"You saved my life," he said.

"You saved mine first," I told him.

His eyebrows pulled together.

I gestured toward the river with my burned hand. "You pulled me out of that mess. I was tangled in a tree stump and caught in some sort of PTSD. I would have drowned if it wasn't for you."

He blinked again and then said. "The mountain lions."

I nodded. "They were possessed by demons. Jumping in the river was the only way we could escape them."

With a grim expression, Vicken pulled up the hem of his shirt and tore a thick strip free. He motioned for the hand I held cradled in my lap.

"You shouldn't have let me drink from you. You're going to be sick," he said levelly as he wrapped my wrist.

"I'd rather be sick than have you dead," I replied. "You need to take better care of yourself."

I realized it was true the moment the words left my mouth. Vicken had been pining after his missing sister and mother. I thought back to the last few days. His clothes hung from a frame that was even more gaunt than usual. His hair was a mess when he usually took a prodigious amount of care about the way he looked. He barely spoke except to snap at me, and even Lorne and Jean had left their coven during lunch to sit with us.

"You need to take care of yourself so we can find your sister," I told him. "And you know your dad is doing everything he can to find your mother. They're going to be alright."

He let out a breath, lowering his walls. "How can you be so sure." He looked forlorn sitting there with my blood staining his chin, his eyes filled with tears, and his clothes still soaking wet from the river.

I gave him what he needed to hear. "Because I won't stop until they are safe."

That brought a slight smile to his lips. "Now you plan to rescue my mother, too?"

"If need be," I replied. I rose and held out a hand. "I'll do whatever it takes to keep our team safe."

He accepted my hand and stood. It filled me with relief to see him steady again.

"I will, too," he replied. "We'd better go make sure they made it to the Academy."

I buttoned the trench coat to keep out the draft and give me at least some semblance of modesty as we hurried through the forest. The dawn light guided us until we could see the spires of the Academy above the trees.

"It's about time," Vicken breathed.

At my questioning look, he said, "I thought we would be stuck out here forever."

"I could track us back to Haunted High, you know," I reminded him.

He glanced at me. "I just didn't want to wait for whenever the moonlight felt like making you a wolf again."

I didn't think he meant it as a jab, but my inability to control my phasing was a sore point. I brooded about it in silence as we made our way back to the school.

I sucked in a breath when I stepped on yet another twig.

"Hold on," I called out.

Vicken watched me pulled the stick out of the bottom of my foot.

"You really shouldn't go into a forest without shoes on," Vicken pointed out.

I rolled my eyes at him and started walking again. "You must be feeling better if you're making jokes."

He nodded. "I told my coven that werewolf blood was like drinking from a dog, but I was wrong. I feel great."

I refrained from asking him how he knew what drinking from a dog was like and went with, "I'm glad to hear it."

He glanced at me. "But you look terrible. How are you feeling?"

"I'll survive," I replied. I could feel the effects of giving him blood taking hold. Along with the lightheadedness, chills were running up and down my body. I pushed myself with the knowledge that if I stopped, we would be stuck in the forest until I recovered. The thought of the cougars happening upon us was enough to keep me placing one foot in front of the other.

Relief filled me when we reached the Academy. Vicken shoved the door with his shoulder, but it didn't budge. He tried the doorknob. "It's not locked," he said with confusion.

We looked at each other and at the same time said, "Brack."

Chapter Twelve

"HE MUST HAVE BEEN worried the cougars would reach the door," Vicken said. He pounded on it with his fists. "Brack, let us in!" he shouted.

I gave a few weak pounds and then leaned against the wall.

Vicken paused and asked, "Finn, are you alright?"

"I don't feel so good," I admitted.

Vicken increased his pounding until dents showed in the metal door.

"Coming!" a voice called.

"They're coming," I told the vampire.

I leaned my head back against the cool bricks and closed my eyes. If I concentrated, I found that standing that way didn't take much effort.

"Brack-warlock, remove the spell," I heard Lyris say from the other side of the door.

"It's gone," Brack replied.

I swore his deep voice reverberated through the bricks into my skull.

The door swung open and would have hit me if Vicken didn't grab it.

"Are you guys alright?" Dara asked. "Professor Briggs told us to seal the door and then went to help with Mercer...."

Her voice faded away when Vicken ducked under my arm and helped me inside.

"What happened?" Lyris demanded.

"He gave me blood," Vicken replied.

"You drank his blood?" Dara said in dismay. I felt her cool hand touch my forehead. "His body's in shock. He needs to rest or it'll start shutting down." She touched my wrist. "It hurts."

"I know it hurts," Vicken snapped. "I did it to him, remember?"

"Maybe you should remember that he's your friend," Alden pointed out.

"Maybe you shouldn't have led us into a death trap in that demon lair in the first place," Vicken shot back.

"Everyone remain calm," Lyris said. "Let's get him up to bed. Vicken-vampire, you look like you could use some rest, also."

"Why are you wet?" Brack asked when he took Vicken's place under my arm. Bandages covered his chest, but I was glad to see that the wounds from the cougars appeared superficial.

"It-it's a long story," I replied.

It took all of my focus to keep my head up enough that I could see where we were going. I stumbled on the stairs, but the warlock held me up easily. By the time we reached the dorms, I was leaning nearly all of my weight on him, but Brack didn't act as though he felt it.

"Right in here," Alden said.

I sunk gratefully onto my bed.

"Is Mercer going to be alright?" I asked.

"Professor Briggs told us that he had to have a lot of stitches. Dr. Six put him in a crystal coma to help him heal faster," Lyris replied.

"Maybe you should take off that wet coat so you don't freeze to death," Dara said, her voice gentle. Her fingers worked at the buttons.

I put a hand on hers. "It's all-all I'm wearing," I replied through chattering teeth.

A blush of embarrassment ran across the empath's face.

"I-I'll get my pajamas on and climb in bed when you leave," I told her to save her from further awkwardness.

She nodded quickly and moved to the door. "Get some sleep," she said.

Lyris smiled at me. "I'll be in with some salves later to help those bruises."

I looked down to see angry black and purple marks across my chest from the stump in the water.

"Thanks," I told her. "Your salves really help."

She gave me a pleased look and joined Dara at the door.

As soon as they left, I reached for my pajama pants. My hand brushed something next to my bed. I looked down to see a corner of silver protruding from beneath the blanket. My heart slowed when I pulled it out to find that my phone was shattered.

"I'm so sorry!"

Alden stood next to me with his gaze on the phone.

"I was straightening up and heard something fall to the floor." His head hung when he said, "I stepped on it by

155

accident before I realized what it was. I didn't mean to break it."

I stared at the phone in my hand. With numb fingers, I opened it to find that the screen was completely broken and the numbers failed to light up when I pushed them. The cellphone didn't respond when I pressed the power button.

"I really am sorry," Alden apologized again.

I nodded wordlessly and slid beneath the blankets. The thought that my lifeline to Dad, Drake, and Julianne was gone hurt almost as badly as the achiness I felt from the vampire bite.

"It's okay," I mumbled. I closed my eyes with the intention of sleeping until the following week.

"Why do cats always land on their feet?"

My eyes flew open at the sound of Professor Briggs' voice. I blinked blearily at the candlelight that filled the classroom. I glanced over to find Dara and Lyris watching me. Sympathy showed on Lyris' face; I couldn't read Dara's expression.

"How did I get here?" I whispered.

"You were here when we got here," Lyris replied in hushed tones.

"You're supposed to be sleeping," Dara pointed out.

"Mr. Briscoe, you haven't answered the question," Professor Briggs said. I heard his limping steps as he made his way to the front of the classroom. "Why do cats always land on their feet?"

I wanted to ask the professor if he knew how I had gotten there, but one look at his face showed that he had no idea what Vicken and I had gone through before we reached the Academy. He apparently thought I was just attending seventh period class like usual at the end of the school day.

I hated the question he asked. It had tormented me since my first day at Haunted High. Black Cat Philosophies had become the class where I was guaranteed to get laughed at no matter what my response. I had tried every answer from scientific to snarky and with the same result. He would tell me I was wrong and then move on with class only to ask me the same question the next day.

My hands balled into fists. I loosened them again immediately at the pain from both of them. I found myself studying the black rag made from Vicken's shirt that was still wrapped where Sparrow should have been. I swallowed against the knot that rose in my throat.

"Mr. Briscoe, do you have an answer?" Professor Briggs pressed.

"Throw me off the roof and I'll figure it out," I replied.

The professor took a limping step forward. "And why is that?" he pressed.

"Because if I was a cat, I would have the instincts not to die," I said.

Silence filled the room. It was broken by the professor's clapping. Confused, I looked up to see him smiling at me. The effect of the candlelight along the scar that marred his cheek was chilling, but his smile softened his appearance.

"Well done, Mr. Briscoe. You gave the right answer."

I stared at him. "You mean you're not going to ask me anymore?"

Laughter sounded from several of the students.

"I'm not going to ask anymore," the professor said. "Instinct is the right answer."

I set my forehead on the table with a loud thump. "I thought it was more complicated than that," I said, my voice muffled.

Professor Briggs gave a quiet chuckle before he replied, "Sometimes all we have to rely on is instinct. For those of us who learn to listen, it's there if we need it, which leads us to our topic today. How do birds fly so close together without running into each other?"

"Instinct," I mumbled.

Laughter rose again from the students around me.

"Yes," Professor Briggs said, "But it goes even deeper than that. Animals have a connection we call...."

"He's asleep."

"I'll take care of him. You three head on to dinner."

"He needs more sleep."

"I'll make sure he gets up to his bed."

The sound of footsteps heading toward the door stole through the last vestiges of my dreamless sleep. I lifted my head, then put a hand to it as a throb of pain made me wish I was asleep again.

"Good morning, or night, I should say," Professor Briggs told me wryly.

I didn't have to open my eyes to recognize the scent of candles. "I'm making a bad habit of sleeping through your class."

"You are," he replied with a hint of humor. "But Vicken told me I should make an exception."

I opened my eyes at that. "He was here?"

Professor Briggs nodded. "Yes, though he looked a bit worse for the wear." He was silent a moment, then said, "The two of you saved our lives."

"The cougars were possessed, like the bear."

Surprise showed on the professor's face. "There was a bear?"

A wry smile touched my lips. "I guess Vicken didn't tell you everything."

"Vampires tend to be a bit closed off," Briggs replied. "Why don't you enlighten me?"

I told him about us running into the demonic bear, casually leaving out the part about our little fight beforehand.

158

When I told of us finally getting it to fall off the cliff, the professor leaned forward from his perch on the edge of a desk.

"Well done," he said. "Sounds like you handled it well."

"That's when we heard Lyris scream," I continued. He knew about how we got the possessed creatures to follow us, but Vicken had apparently also left out our need to jump in the river, him saving my life, and then me in turn letting him drink my blood.

Professor Briggs was silent for a few minutes. His gaze lingered on the black cloth around my wrist. "You let a vampire drink your blood. No wonder you've been sleeping in here like you're dead. You're lucky you're not a ghost following Alden around."

I gave a small chuckle. "Vicken said the same thing when he came to and realized what I had done, or he had done." I rubbed my forehead. "Everything's a bit jumbled right now."

"What you need to do is go to bed for a few days." When I opened my mouth to protest, Professor Briggs cut me off by saying, "I'll write an excuse and have Alden get all of your homework. I'll have Lyris bring up some dinner so you get something in your stomach. You need sleep, plenty of food, more water than you think you can handle, and more sleep. Doctor's orders."

I gave a tired laugh. "I didn't know you were a doctor."

"I'd be teaching at an Ivy League school if I wasn't here," Briggs replied with a straight face. "It's too bad they don't consider Black Cat Philosophies or the History of Witches and Warlocks as thesis material."

"Maybe someday the world will be more open to this kind of stuff," I replied.

A hint of wistfulness appeared and then left his face so quickly I wondered if I had imagined it.

He rose and said, "Let's get you to bed."

I lost track of how much time I spent laying on top of my blankets willing sleep to come. My eyes kept straying to the bandage Lyris had wrapped around my wrist in the place of Vicken's rag. Thoughts of Sparrow's death circled around my mind like a caged bird. I was grateful for the distraction when Alden came in carrying a bowl of soup and several rolls.

"Can't sleep?" he asked when he handed me the bowl.

I shook my head.

He must have seen something in my expression because he said, "I talk to my mom when I'm feeling bad." The Grim suddenly looked up and his cheeks paled. "I'm so sorry," he said. "I forgot that your mom died." He looked at the ground, the foot of my bed, and the ceiling, anywhere but at me, before he continued with, "I don't know what I would do without my mom. She's always been there for me when I need someone to talk to. I just don't know what I would do if I didn't have her."

He walked to the door, then paused and looked back at me. "I'm going to practice chants with Lyris and Brack. Get some sleep."

I stared at the bowl of soup long enough to know exactly how many pieces of chicken, celery, and carrots floated in it. Thanks to Alden's words, the thoughts of my mom came so strongly I could barely breathe. I could see her ghost when she smiled back at me in the upstairs hallway. Because she had passed away when I was so young, her ghost was the closest thing to being around her that I remembered besides snippets of memory and the videos my dad kept.

With the loss of Sparrow, my near-death in the river, and the stress of trying to find the key to her box so that we could figure out what it would take to defeat Chutka the Shambler, my need to see my mother again became so strong I couldn't sit there and do nothing.

I set the uneaten bowl of soup on the floor, slipped on my shoes someone had thoughtfully brought back from the cemetery, and crept to the door. Luckily, my feet were pretty much healed from the moonlight that fell on my bed through the window, and the soles didn't hurt nearly as bad as they had when we first reached the Academy. I peered out, but the halls were mostly empty. Those students who did walk around didn't seem at all concerned about one bedraggled werewolf.

I ran up the stairs until I reached the thirteenth floor. Disappointment filled me when my mother's ghost wasn't in the hallway. I don't know why I had been so certain that she would be there, but the lack of her ghost made me angry in a way I couldn't explain.

I climbed through the window, ran to the end of the roof, and hurried up the invisible staircase. By the time I slid down the slide to the clubhouse, I told myself that she had to be there waiting, she had to know how much I needed her.

The sight of the empty room drove me to my knees. I bent with my hands over my head and tried to hold myself together. I could feel myself slipping over the edge into a dark place I didn't want to visit. I was afraid of the bottomless pit I saw and the thought of what would happen if I truly lost control.

There was another place filled with ghosts. My head lifted at the thought. I slid back up the slide, ran down the staircase, took the Academy's stairs five at a time, and narrowly avoided bowling students over as I made my way to the hallway of doors. Exotic scents filled my nose from doorways I had never visited. I wondered why the Academy used the one door but kept the others locked. The reminder that the forest one was also supposed to be closed whispered in my mind. I ran forward in fear that it would be locked like all the others. To my relief, it stood open a crack. I stepped through with

161

the thought that I should tell Brack to work his spell on it again when I returned.

"Finn, what are you doing here?" Mezania asked when I reached the cemetery.

"Oh, uh, just checking on something," I replied.

I had forgotten that I would need her help to open the tomb. The sight of Sparrow's little ghost sleeping around her wrist nearly made me turn around and head back to the Academy without asking. But I steeled my nerves and said, "Mercer wanted me to see if the demons have calmed down. He's worried about the threat they pose to Haunted High. Can you open it for me?"

I had never been a good liar. Fortunately, I must have been somewhat passable because Mezania nodded. "Of course. Anything for you." She paused, then said, "You brought Trace back to me. The time we have together is so precious. I don't know how I'll ever be able to repay you for that."

The heartache in her voice told of how hard it was for the ghost and the warlock to be apart. I lowered my gaze. "I'm sorry you have to go through this."

Mezania gave a brave little sniff and crossed to the tombstone that made up the entrance to the Otherworld. "I'm just glad I can help in some way."

The tomb slid aside at her touch.

"Be careful down there," she told me. "I'll keep it open in case you need to come back in a hurry."

"Thank you," I replied.

Despite my ability to see in the dark, I found myself missing the flashlights and sounds of footsteps behind me. I hurried down the steps until I felt like I was going back up, and then I reached the ceiling of the Academy's corridor. I crossed quickly through the halls with the hopes of remaining unnoticed. Fortunately, I didn't see the Demon Knight on my way up the stairs. The ghosts and demons below that wandered with the occasional student didn't seem to detect my presence. It was disorienting to run up the sloped ceiling, but I found myself on the thirteenth floor in less time than I thought it would take.

I stopped at the sight of the ghost who stood at the end looking out the window.

"Mom?" I asked.

The ghost turned and smiled my mother's smile. Relief filled me at the sight of her golden hair and the way her eyes, so like mine, echoed her smile when she looked up at me. I walked slowly along the roof toward her. It felt strange to be eye-to-eye, yet for me to feel as if she was upside down when I was the one who walked on the ceiling.

I stopped a few steps away. "I-I've missed you," I told her.

Her voice was warm when she replied, "I've missed you, too. You should stay awhile."

The thought that she wanted me there filled me with happiness. Any doubt I had at coming there vanished.

"Are you alright?" I asked. "Are you happy?"

She nodded and the ghostly glow that surrounded her brightened. "I am happy, but I miss you."

"I miss you, too," another voice whispered.

I looked around, but couldn't see anyone.

"It's been hard at the Academy," I told her. "Everyone's afraid of werewolves, I lost Sparrow to the Demon Knight," I held out my hand to show her the dragon's absence that ate at me. "And everything seems to be against me figuring out how to stop more demons from reaching the school."

A whisper in my own voice said, "Reaching the school."

I put it off as an echo in the strange world and said, "Thanks for telling me about the clubhouse. We found what we were looking for."

"You did?" she replied, her eyes bright. "What did you find?"

"What did you find?" a voice repeated.

I looked around, but even though I had the distinct sensation that we were being watched, I couldn't see anyone.

I shrugged uneasily and said, "You know. The mark under the table."

My mom nodded. "Yes, the mark." She paused, then said, "Which one was it?"

Uneasiness filled me. I watched her carefully when I replied, "The mark of Chutka the Shambler. The one that you put there."

"Yes, that one," she said. She smiled warmly. "You're so smart. I knew you could find it."

I toyed with the bandaged on my wrist when I told her, "It led me to the box, but I don't have the key. Do you know where I can find it?"

She smiled again. "Keys are important, but they are also dangerous. You should probably just leave it alone."

"Leave it alone," came the whisper.

I spun in a circle. "Who said that?" I demanded.

No one stood behind me even though when the voice spoke, the hair had stood up on the back of my neck at the hot breath that washed across my skin.

I glanced back at my mother's ghost. "What's going on here?"

She shook her head and her hair swayed softly in a current I couldn't see. "I don't know, but I want you to be safe. You should forget about the key and stay here with me."

The thought of staying with my mom was a comforting one. My weary mind welcomed the chance to rest under the watchful gaze of someone who cared about me.

Mom reached out a hand. "Stay with me, Finn. You'll be happier here."

I stretched out my hand toward her and then paused. Something was wrong. Briggs' conversation with Mezania lingered in my mind. He wanted to stay with her, but Mezania loved him too much to let him throw his life away early. My mother would want me to live my life, not give up and stay in some half-world with her. I pulled my hand back.

"What's wrong, Finn?" she asked. "Don't you want to stay with me?"

I saw it then, the flicker in her eyes that wasn't part of the green irises we shared. I took a step back. Something the Grims had told Headmistress Wrengold before they left surfaced in my mind. The ghosts weren't able to talk to us or respond because they were reliving memories of their past. That was why my mother had told me the rhyme to get to the clubhouse. She wasn't talking to me, she was reliving a moment in her life when she had repeated the rhyme over and over in order to remember it.

The ghost before me wasn't my mother. She was a demon sent by Chutka the Shambler, who was pleased I knew his name. A chill ran down my spine at the truth of the thought. I took another step backwards.

"Don't go, Finn. We have so much to talk about," not-Mom's ghost said.

"I'm done talking," I replied.

I spun and ran for the hallway with the fear that the imposter ghost would follow me and find a way to keep me in the Otherworld forever.

I turned a corner and ran into something so hard I fell back several steps.

Chapter Thirteen

"VICKEN!" I SAID IN surprise.

"Finn!" he exclaimed with equal shock on his face. "What are you doing here?"

"I was talking to a ghost I thought was my mom, but turned out not to be, and now I think she's going to try to keep me here."

"Naturally," Vicken replied. "It might be because we're here talking on the ceiling of a shadow version of Haunted High, but that actually makes sense. Come on."

We took off running down the ceiling of the stairs.

"What are you doing here?" I asked. I knew the answer before the question left my mouth, so I finished with, "Did you find your sister?"

"No," he replied as we ran through the corridor. "I thought I'd search everywhere I had seen her, but there are too many demons."

"And they've seen you?" I asked in shock.

"What do you think?" Vicken replied.

We both slowed to a stop. My heart beat louder at the sight of dozens of demons waiting for us in front of the stairway. I glanced back and saw not-Mom's ghost walk down the last step.

"Come on, Finn," she called. "Stay here with me."

Vicken looked back at me. "That's just creepy."

"Tell me about it," I replied. "Come on. We've got to find somewhere to hide."

We took off up the stairs again.

"What places have you checked for Amryn?" I asked him as we ran.

"I started with the thirteenth floor because of the entrance to the secret passage, and then I was going to check—"

"Her room," I finished. We stared at each other wide-eyed. It was the last place I had smelled her scent. I took off up the stairway to the fifth floor. We ran down the hallway and skidded to a stop in front of room E twenty-five. Her scent was strong.

"I think she's in there," I whispered to Vicken.

Fear showed in his gaze. "What if she's not?"

"Then we'll keep searching until we find her," I replied firmly. I leaned down and grabbed the doorknob. With a silent plea, I pushed the door open.

"Vicken!"

Amryn's voice and the answering look on her brother's face gripped my heart in a fist.

Vicken ran inside. "I've been looking everywhere for you," he said with tears in his eyes as he gathered his sister up in his arms. "I would never give up. You know I wouldn't."

"I know, I know," she sobbed against his chest. Her long dark hair hid her face from view as she clung to him. "I just knew you would find me."

He held her back at arm's length. "Are you alright?"

She nodded. "Just scared, really, really scared." Tears fell down her cheeks. "I want to go home."

Footsteps sounded below.

"We've got to go," I told them.

Vicken took Amryn's hand. "I'll never let go, alright?"

She nodded. "Me neither."

He gave her a reassuring smile and she took a calming breath. She nodded at me. "Let's get out of here."

We sprinted down the hallway and paused at the staircase, but no one was there. At my motion, the two vampires followed me down the stairs. We stopped at every hallway and checked, but no demons or even ghosts showed up. By the time we reached the main corridor, my nerves felt like glass. I was sure we were running into an ambush set by either the not-Mom ghost or the demons who had been waiting for Vicken to return.

The sight of the empty corridor made my blood run cold.

"Where are they all?" I asked.

"Who cares," Vicken replied. "Let's get out of here before they figure out we're gone."

I couldn't argue with that. I led the way up the dark staircase with the vampires close behind. Vicken kept a hand on my shoulder as we ran. When Amryn stumbled, he picked her up on his back and practically flew up the stairs after me.

I burst out into the moonlight and paused at the sight of Mezania sitting on her tombstone.

"Where did they go?" I asked her.

"Who?" she replied, baffled.

"The demons," I said with exasperation. I gestured toward the tombstone. "Where did the demons go?"

She shook her head. "I haven't seen any demons. You went down there and then Vicken, but nobody else. You're the only ones I've seen come back up."

It made no sense. "Will you shut the tomb?" I asked her, then I took off running for the Academy.

I could hear Vicken and Amryn following behind at a slower pace, but instincts drove me on. I barely slowed when I barreled through the door, then I kept on running. Too many students were in the corridor for me to safely use the passage behind the unicorn painting, so I was forced to run up the stairs. A strange sense of deja vu filled me when I reached the top. I slid my hand along the opposite wall for the trigger, then darted through the opening into the dark passage beyond.

By the time I shoved the door open to the basement, I felt like my heart was going to burst out of my chest. I met the wide eyes of my teammates as I gasped for breath.

"Finn, you're supposed to be resting!" Dara said.

"Looks like he's doing anything but that," Briggs said with a look of disapproval on his face.

"Wait," I gasped. "I need...I need to know how to tell...."

I sucked in a breath in an attempt not to pass out. I put my hands on my knees.

Professor Briggs must have seen something in my expression because he crossed to me and set a hand on my back. "Take your time. Breathe. You can ask us anything, but we need to be able to understand you."

I felt it the moment Dara set a hand on my arm. My panicked breathing slowed and my thundering heartbeat eased. The fears that had pressed against me faded until I could think again. I rose and sucked in a calming breath.

"Thank you," I told her.

She nodded. "What was that?"

I couldn't decide where to start. I went with, "How can I tell if one of our team is actually a demon?"

Everyone looked at each other.

"Really," I said. "We have a very serious problem."

"Who do you think is the demon?" Professor Briggs asked levelly.

I pointed at Alden.

Everyone stared at the Grim with wide eyes.

"Me?" he said. The hurt in his gaze ate at me, but I didn't take back the accusation.

"Where are your ghosts, Alden?" I asked him. "I haven't seen them around in a while."

"I told you. They realized I can't help them like my parents can and got bored of following me around," he replied, rising from the wooden table.

"What about destroying my cellphone and you talking about your mother like I'm missing out on something important?" My voice threatened to catch, but I pushed through it. "You wanted to destroy any contact I had with my family so I would search for Mom in the one place I knew I could find her. You almost had me trapped in the Otherworld without a way to get back. If it wasn't for the fact that she didn't know about Chutka's mark, I might have fallen for it." I raced through the thoughts that had spurred me on since we came out of the tombstone. "What about dropping the flashlight that alerted the Demon Knight? What about that?" I demanded. "You're the reason Sparrow died!"

My chest was heaving. Professor Briggs stood between me and the small Grim. Alden's innocent light blue eyes didn't fool me.

"Slow down," the professor told me. "You're accusing Alden of being a demon?"

"I know he's a demon," I replied. "I just need to prove it. Lyris, Brack, isn't there a chant or something you can do?"

Lyris gave Professor Briggs an anxious look. "Not that we know."

Briggs shook his head. "There's nothing like that."

I decided to play the last hand I had. "Vicken and I found Amryn."

The briefest flicker of green fire surfaced in Alden's gaze, then vanished just as quickly.

"There! Did you see it?" I exclaimed. "Did you see the demon fire?"

My teammates exchanged glances. I could tell nobody believed me.

"Finn, calm down," the professor said. "Did you really find Amryn?"

I nodded. "We went back to the Otherworld and searched until we found her in her room, but when we brought her out, the demons were gone."

Professor Briggs' eyes widened. "Gone? All of them?"

I nodded. "Every single one." I pointed an accusing finger at Alden. "And he knows where they've gone."

"You know me," Alden said with hurt in his voice. "How can you accuse me of something so horrible?" His voice deepened when he asked, "How can you think something so appalling about a friend of yours?" His face twisted until it was unrecognizable. "And such a good friend at that?"

I fought back the urge to cower away from the vehemence that had taken over Alden's voice. I clenched my hands into fists and stood firm. "Who are you and what have you done with my friend?"

Alden's hands lifted to his face. He began pulling off shreds of skin. Everyone backed away in horror. He covered his face and let out a shriek, bending over until his elbows were on his knees.

"Alden?" Lyris asked with fear in her voice.

"I'm not Alden," he replied in a deep voice I recognized.

"Back away!" I told my team.

"What's going on?" Vicken asked from the stairs.

"Stay back," Briggs told him.

As the being raised his head, he grew. The shadows of the room gathered around him as though drawn to his dark soul. By the time the Dark Knight stood at full height, he towered over even Brack. Other shadows appeared in the room; demons began to pour from the walls as though they had been waiting for the Knight to reveal himself.

"Keep staring, little werewolf," he said in a thundering voice. "You've already failed to protect this school."

Screams rang out up the stairs. I took a step toward the door, but I had no idea what to do. Did I leave my team with the Dark Knight and run up to protect the rest of the students with what little I could do against the demons, or did I stay and pit myself against one of Chutka the Shambler's subordinates?

"Save them," a voice whispered next to me. "They're all dying."

I glanced over but no one was there. I gritted my teeth and stood still. "What do you want from us?" I demanded.

Glee showed in the Knight's burning eyes. "I don't want anything from you," he said.

While the Demon Knight spoke, Professor Briggs began silently moving my team toward the door and away from him.

I moved so that the Knight's attention stayed on me as he continued with, "I want my demons to become you, to possess you until they know how you think, how you act, and how you feel. I want them to infiltrate your families and pretend to be a part of them until I am ready for them to take over and destroy the mythics completely."

It was the same thing Lyris had told us, yet it still didn't make any sense to me. "Why?"

"To see the world cower in fear from Prince Chutka. Chaos upon chaos, betrayal and fear in the streets and terror in the homes of both humans and mythic-kind." The Demon Knight's sharp-toothed mouth widened behind the hole in his helm. "A world ruled by demons is a beautiful thought indeed."

I studied his armor as he spoke. The dark plates slid together when he moved. But where the sound of metal on metal should have been, only silence reached my ears. I looked for chinks in his armor, for anything that would give me hope that I could beat him. My eyes lingered on the center of his chest. The armor looked misshapen there with a mark that looked vaguely like...a key! My heart leaped into my throat.

I heard Brigg's voice again when he said, "They must be using an object to let themselves into our world, something from here but not of here."

"You have a very twisted view of this world, Knight," I said as I thought quickly.

"The world is already twisted, werewolf," the Demon Knight replied. "It needs only a nudge to fall off the edge completely."

Briggs silently stood in front of the door and motioned the girls to go out behind him.

"I don't believe you," I said to keep the Demon Knight occupied.

"Would you believe that your little attempt to distract me has failed?" the Demon Knight replied.

He raised his hand toward the door. Dara let out a scream as she was lifted into the air. Her back arched and she shrieked in pain.

"No!" Briggs shouted.

He lifted his cane and pointed it at the Demon Knight. At a single word from the professor, orange flame ran down the length of the walking stick. He swung it at the Knight as if it was a sword.

The Demon Knight's attention broke from Dara when he turned to defend himself. Brack lunged forward and caught the empath before she could hit the ground. The Knight opened his hand with a flourish. His fingers grew into thin, pointed swords that he used to block Briggs' advances.

"Get up the stairs!" I called to my teammates.

Briggs let out a cry of pain and stumbled. Brack pulled him back against the door. The warlock's hand showed red when he took it away from the professor's side. Brack helped him onto the stairs and stood in the way so the Demon Knight couldn't get to him.

The three vampires attacked. I had never seen such fast movement as Vicken, Lorne, and Jean fought with daggers they pulled from their sleeves. I wondered if Mercer had treated them with poison as he had promised to do when they were done training, but by the reaction from the Demon Knight, their attacks were only making him more angry.

"Lorne!" Vicken shouted an instant before the Demon Knight shoved his five finger blades into the vampire's chest.

Vicken and Jean fought with desperation to save their friend. I lunged in front of Lorne and pulled him back toward the door. Jean let out a cry of pain and fell to the floor clutching his thigh. Vicken grabbed his friend and hauled him back.

Red colored my vision at the sight of my teammates bleeding on the stairs. Dara and Lyris did what they could to bind the wounds, but by the pallor of Lorne's face, I knew he didn't have much time left.

The Demon Knight laughed. "Your attempts to stop me are pathetic. Give up now or lose more of your friends!"

The demons behind him laughed with cruel cackles.

"Shut the door, Brack!" I shouted over the demons' mocking laughter.

"What about you?" the huge warlock asked with fear on his face.

"They'll have to go through me to get up those stairs."

"They'll have to go through us," Lyris said. She and Dara climbed carefully over the wounded and made their way out the door.

Vicken followed close behind. "Through us," he repeated.

"Shut the door so none of the demons can get up the stairs," I ordered.

Brack made the door slam shut and stood in front of it, trapping us inside the basement with the demon horde and their cruel leader.

"Begin the chant," Vicken said.

Lyris and Brack spoke the foreign words aloud. A shimmering golden orb surrounded us, attesting to how much stronger they had gotten since they last used the chant. But the iridescent bubble looked frail compared to the glowing eyes and reaching claws of the demons behind the Knight.

The Demon Knight advanced. I glanced around quickly for any possible weapon. With Briggs injured and Jean trying desperately to patch up both Lorne and the professor, it was just myself, Vicken, Lyris, Dara, and Brack standing in the way of a demon horde ready to take over Haunted High. I wondered briefly how I had gotten myself into such a situation.

The demons began to spit flames from their mouths and nostrils. The green fire grew, roaring over them as they waited behind the Demon Knight with an eerie calm. The flames raced up the Knight's armor until he glowed with the intensity. I glanced at Vicken and saw the desperate fear on his face. There was no way we could survive so much fire.

I looked away from him and my eyes landed on the Mercer's box in the corner.

"I have an idea," I told the others.

"Don't leave the shield," Vicken said, his yellow eyes wide. "You'll die out there!"

"Protect the others," I commanded. "I'll be back."

I stepped through the orb and took off running the moment my shoes touched the ground. There was a small path between the demons and the wall. I told myself that if I kept to it, I would be safe from the fire. The green flames immediately lapped at my shoes, proving me wrong.

I told myself with each step that the fire couldn't hurt me. It had no power if I didn't let it overcome my self-control. But man did it hurt.

I slid to a stop next to the box and threw the lid open. I picked up the smaller box inside and withdrew the always-lit candle without bothering to use Mercer's special tongs. The fire spilled over my arms as I ran back toward the shield. I bit my tongue as I leaped over the outstretched claws of demons who lay waiting to snag me on my way past. I fumbled the candle once, but managed to catch it before it could hit the ground. Luckily, the Demon Knight appeared content to watch my pathetic attempt at survival and didn't stop me when I leaped back inside the orb.

"What are you doing?" Vicken asked. He shied away from the green flame I held as if it was as deadly as the fire outside the shield.

"Fighting fire with fire," I said.

"What are you talking about?" Dara asked.

Lyris and Brack watched me with wide eyes as they chanted in unison.

"We're going to die, right?" I asked them. I looked at each of their faces in turn and saw that they knew the same thing. "I say we give it one last shot." I swallowed as what I was about to ask them to do went far beyond the scope of a team. "I need you guys to trust me."

The warlock and witch nodded with fear bright on their faces.

"We trust you," Dara said. Her voice shook only slightly as she looked from me to the demons waiting just outside the shield.

I held Vicken's gaze. The vampire looked from me to the flame, then nodded. "I trust you." The fear in his eyes told how hard the words were, but his voice didn't waver.

I threw the candle to the floor. The green flames raced along our feet and up our legs.

Lyris screamed and Brack's arms lowered. The shield wavered.

"Don't lose your concentration!" I yelled.

They began chanting again. Lyris closed her eyes as tears streamed down her cheeks. Dara winced as the pain of the flames intensified.

I grabbed Vicken's shaking arm and pointed to the key engraved into the Demon Knight's chest plate.

"That's what we're looking for!" I shouted above the roar of the flames. "It's our only chance!"

The fire I had started rose higher.

"You've killed yourself," the Demon Knight said with a grin of triumph. The flames from his demon horde danced all over him with such a bright green light I could barely look in his direction. "How sweet to choose suicide as a team rather than death by my demons. Though you won't stop us from reaching your families. You're only delaying the inevitable."

"Finn?" Dara shouted as the flames reached even higher.

"On the count of three, drop the shield and join hands," I told them. I met Dara's gaze. "I'm going to need your help."

She nodded with tears in her eyes at the pain of the flames.

My gaze shifted to Vicken. "Hold her other hand and don't let go no matter what, understand?"

The vampire nodded. His face was white with shock at the fire that covered his legs up to his waist.

"One," I called. I could barely breathe past the pain of the flames that crawled up my shirt. "Two," the Demon Knight stepped closer, intent on finishing us the moment the shield was down. "Three!" I shouted.

Lyris and Brack stopped chanting together and the golden orb vanished. The fire from the demons surged forward, but met the roar of the fire I had started and was repelled. I grabbed Dara's hand and lunged toward the Demon Knight. The moment I set my hand on his chest plate, it felt like my fingers, wrist, and arm melted away. I realized my mistake in grabbing Dara with my left hand and using my right against the flame, but I didn't have a chance to switch it without risking everyone. Dara gasped at the force of the pain, but she held fast, pulling what she could from me so that I could stand it.

I gritted my teeth and reached for the key. The Demon Knight didn't realize what I was doing until my fingers brushed the imprint. But I couldn't quite reach it. I leaned forward, worried that he would step back out of my grasp and I would lose my only chance. In a moment of desperation, I let go of Dara's hand and grabbed the key with my good hand. A shout of pain tore from my lips when my fingers closed around the burning key. I felt hands grab my shoulders. The pain lessened as I was yanked backwards. I fell into the circle of my friends. The fire roared around us, demons hissed and clawed at the imitation flames, and the eyes of the Demon Knight followed me as I landed on my knees on the flaming ground.

Afraid that I had failed, I opened my hand slowly. The silver key sat on my burned palm; the bright metal glittered in the green firelight. We all looked from the key on my palm to the Demon Knight. His green flame eyes narrowed, then widened at what he saw. He reached up and touched the hole in his chest where the key had been.

I held the key up. "Leave our school and never return!" I shouted.

The knight clawed at the hole in his chest. The hole widened until it was larger than his head, then he began to collapse inward. A strange shrieking noise sounded as the Demon Knight's arms and legs were pulled in followed by his torso, his shoulders, and finally his head. There was a sickening pop as the last of him turned inside-out and then vanished.

The demons who had filled the room behind the Demon Knight scrambled backwards in fear. As we watched, their fires went out and they retreated to the shadows. Their bodies became insubstantial and they were sucked back through the bricks of the basement as though they were being pulled by a giant vacuum. Within seconds, the demons had vanished completely.

Vicken used his cloak to smother the flames of the fire I had lit. While there was relief on his face, the tightness of his gaze and the way his hands shook as he got rid of the last of the fire told just how hard standing there had been on him.

Lyris and Brack dropped to their knees as soon as the fire was gone. Dara and I supported each other, our chests heaving and hands remembering the pain of the fire that had tried to devour us. Yet when I looked at my right hand that held the key, it hadn't been damaged any further by the flame.

Chapter Fourteen

"YOU DID IT," DARA said.

"We did it," I replied.

"Using the imitation fire to block the demon fire was brilliant," Vicken said. "But could you warn us next time? That wasn't pleasant."

"At least we're alive," Dara pointed out.

An eerie glow still filled the room. As my eyes adjusted to the new darkness, I made out the forms of ghosts, hundreds of them, packed within the basement.

"W-what are they doing?" Lyris asked.

"I'm not sure," I replied.

I moved Dara behind me and took a step forward.

The ghosts parted to reveal the vampire ghost I had met in the infirmary. He held up the box that had come from the one in our attic marked with the sigil of Chutka the Shambler.

"I was wrong about your friends," he said in the low voice I remembered. "They protected you as you protected them. Well done."

He carried the box to me. I accepted it cautiously, sure he would turn into the demon once more.

"The demons are gone for now," he said as if he had read my thoughts. "In the box you will find one part of a key to defeat Chutka the Shambler and end the threat he poses to your world."

"Not another key," I groaned.

The ghost smiled a toothy smile. "Of a sort. Good luck, Mr. Briscoe."

"Thank you," I replied.

The ghosts stepped back. I set the box on the table, only then noticing how my hands shook. I glanced back at my team and saw the same relieved, exhausted expressions on their faces that I knew showed on mine. Brack had opened the door to let Dara and Lyris tend to our wounded. Professor Briggs leaned against the door frame with a hand on his side. He gave me a reassuring nod.

I put the key in the lock and turned it. The box opened. I peered inside and was disappointed to see that the only thing inside was what looked like a small black rock.

"That's it," Professor Briggs said. He limped up behind me. "That's what your uncle used to open the gateway to the demons. I thought it was gone forever. Your mother must have locked it away to protect the school when she left."

I studied the lump. "What is it?"

"A piece of Chutka's heart," the vampire ghost replied. "Guard it well for he is as desperate to get it back as you are to finish him. There are two more pieces. Put them together and then destroy them once and for all."

"Where do we find the other pieces?" Vicken asked.

The ghost shook his head. "That I do not know. I wish you luck. You have my respect, Finnley Briscoe." The vampire ghost gave a sweeping bow and faded from sight.

The other ghosts did the same, vanishing until it was just my team in the basement.

I shut the lid of the box and locked it again, then withdrew the key.

"I'll take that for safe keeping," Professor Briggs said.

I held out the box. When he reached for his, he winced and grabbed his side.

"You can have it if I can help you to the infirmary," I told him.

"Deal," he replied with a pained expression.

Brack carried Lorne while Lyris and Dara helped Jean up the stairs. Professor Briggs lasted about three steps before his hold on his cane faltered. He would have fallen if I hadn't caught him.

"Enough of this," I told him.

Before he could protest, I ducked under his arms and picked him up.

"Put me down," Briggs commanded.

I ignored him and started up the stairs. "You really think you can make it up from the basement to the second floor in your condition? It would take two days."

He rolled his eyes. "I'm fine, Finn. I can walk."

I paused and gave him a steeling look. "Are you going to protect that box or bleed out on these stairs? The way I see it, those are the only two options right now." I smothered the fact that the amount of blood that covered his side and dripped onto the stairs alarmed me more than I let on.

Briggs must have seen it in my face anyway because he nodded. "Fine, but you can't tell anyone about this."

"I won't," I replied.

While Mercer didn't exactly look happy to see us, he grunted at the sight of our team together in the infirmary. The bandages across his torso showed blood, and when he moved, he gave an uncharacteristic grunt of pain.

I crossed to his bed.

"Looks like it went well," he said dryly.

I held out the key. "We got what we needed, but we're not done. Briggs has the box with the piece of Chutka's heart, but there are two more we need to find."

Mercer shifted uncomfortably on the bed. "I feared as much. Keep the key. It should be separate from the box."

I withdrew my hand. "Lyris said Briggs is going to be okay, but Lorne and Jean need surgery. Dr. Six says she's bringing in help. Keep an eye on them for me."

"Where are you going?" the sweeper asked with suspicion in his gaze.

"To find Alden," I replied.

I hurried back down the stairs, but my steps faltered. I leaned against the railing for a moment to give my head a chance to stop spinning.

Footsteps came up behind me.

"You push yourself too hard," Dara said. She set a hand on my shoulder. "You're going to be of no use to anyone if you don't get some food in you, especially after giving so much blood to Vicken."

I allowed her to help me up. "But I need to find Alden. I think he's waiting for me."

Dara read the determination on my face. "I'll grab something from the cafeteria and meet you in the forest. Will that work?"

Relief filled me at her understanding. "That would be great."

We walked together down the stairs and then she left me to head to the hallway of doors. I passed scents that intrigued

184

me, but kept my focus on the one that was open. I had no idea who had unlocked it originally after Brack left, but I was grateful it remained open just the same.

I stepped into the forest and let out a sigh at the feeling of sunshine on my shoulders. I wanted to run to the cemetery, but the thought of Dara finding me passed out along the way kept me from pushing myself. By the time she caught up to me, I felt stronger from the warmth of the sun's rays. The scent of the crisp mountain breeze brought with it hints of frosted pines from higher up on the mountain. I fought back the urge to phase and explore it.

"I found pulled pork rolls and cooked hamburger patties. I figured you needed protein," Dara said when she caught up to me. "But first, drink some water."

I fought back a grin at her orders and did as I was told. I drained the first water bottle she held out, then chuckled and accepted the second one. I finished it just as quickly.

"Good. Now eat all of this. You're not going to help Alden if you don't listen to me," she said, softening her chiding tone with a teasing wink.

I didn't tell her that the thought of not listening had never crossed my mind. I ate the pulled pork rolls and cold hamburger patties with relish at the flavor, the way my stomach filled, and the taste of something besides the ash that had lingered in my mouth since the demon fire. The food tasted better than anything I could remember, and I finished it before we had even reached the cemetery.

"It's so beautiful here," Dara said.

Finally feeling more like myself, I was taken by the way the dapple light from between the leaves danced across her face, catching in her ashen hair and making her violet eyes glow.

"It is," I replied with my eyes on her instead of the forest.

"A beautiful place to be buried," she said.

185

I was caught off-guard by her words. "What?"

I followed her gaze and saw that we had reached the cemetery. The realization of why we were there pressed against me, and with it returned the desperate need to find Alden and ensure that he was safe.

"Mezania, can you open the tomb?" I asked.

"Of course," the ghost replied.

I lingered by her tombstone and Sparrow's ghost, but the little dragon watched Mezania as though she didn't see me. It made my heart hurt.

As soon as the dark stairway was revealed, I started down it.

"Finn?" Dara said hesitantly behind me.

I looked back to see that she had followed me down, but with the thick darkness, she was forced to take the steps much more slowly.

"I've got you," I said.

I ran back up to her and slipped my hand in hers. Warmth ran up my arm at her touch. Before I could allow myself to get lost in being so close to her, I forced myself to continue down.

"I keep trying to think about the last time I saw him with ghosts following him," I told her to keep my mind distracted. "I figure that was the last time he was really himself."

"The ghosts followed him to the clubhouse," she said.

I nodded. "But they were gone when I woke up in the cemetery." A thought occurred to me and I paused in the upside-down corridor. "I think I saw them last while he was sleeping. I'll bet he's in our room!"

We took off running up the stairs. On the third floor, we ran to dorm thirty-three. I opened the door and pushed it inward. My heart slowed at the sight of Alden curled into a ball in the corner of the ceiling. He looked like he was sleeping.

Figures in white surrounded his still form. They turned at my entrance. I didn't know whether to be afraid or if they were harmless; either way, I pulled Dara behind me to keep her safe.

"Why are you here?" I asked.

An older woman with kind eyes smiled at me. "Grims take care of the spirits of those who pass away. It is a hard job, but they are never alone."

"You're watching over him?" I said. My muscles loosened at the realization that they didn't mean him harm.

"Of course," a man with short gray hair and a warm smile told us. "Family takes care of family."

"You're all Grims," Dara said with awe from behind me.

They nodded as a group. "And now we'll leave him in your capable hands," the first woman said. She gave me a warm smile. "We're glad he has you. Werewolves make loyal friends."

Twinkling lights filled the air so bright Dara and I had to shield our eyes with our hands. When the light faded, Alden was left alone.

I dropped to my knees next to him. "Alden, wake up," I said. I shook his shoulder gently.

"Finn?" Alden lifted his head and gave me an unfocused look. "Is that really you?"

I nodded and couldn't fight back the smile that spread across my face. "It's really me."

Alden rose and hugged me so tight I could barely believe the strength in his small body.

"I was sleeping and I couldn't wake up," he said. I felt tears soak my shirt when he continued with, "I kept doing bad things, but I couldn't stop myself, even when the team was in danger, I couldn't control what was happening. It was horrible!"

"Everything's alright now," I told him. I patted his back. "Haunted High is safe, our team is recuperating, and everyone is going to be fine."

Alden cried as if he couldn't stop. I met Dara's gaze. She nodded and set a hand on his shoulder.

"It's alright," she said in a voice just above a whisper. "Breathe, Alden. You didn't do anything wrong."

His sobs slowed and then stopped with the empath's help. Finally, Alden lifted his head and gave us both a watery smile. "Are you sure?"

We nodded in unison.

A sigh of relief came from the Grim before he sat up.

"Alden, what's that on your arm?" Dara asked.

Light showed from beneath Alden's sleeve. He pulled it back and everyone stared.

"Mezania Brown," he said, reading the first name that glowed blue on his forearm. Then he said, "Sparrow."

The names made my heart clench in pain. I looked at him in an effort to distract my thoughts. "I thought Grims didn't escort animals."

He gave me a small smile. "No one crosses over alone. Other spirits are there to walk with the gentle creatures of this world. But you're right when you say that Grims don't normally do it." He pushed his pale hair back from his face and said, "Sparrow sacrificed herself for you. There is a very special place for creatures like her, and I get to be the one to help her find it."

My eyes burned but I blinked quickly to keep the tears from falling.

"She deserves that," I said.

"She does," Dara agreed.

Together, we walked up the stairs. I don't think any of us were surprised to see Professor Briggs already at the cemetery. Briggs leaned against Mezania's tombstone with a hand on his side as they spoke. When we left the pit beneath the demon gateway, he and Mezania turned to us with warm smiles.

"I'm glad to see you're alright," the professor told Alden.

"Thank you," Alden replied. But he lowered his head as though he couldn't bring himself to say the words he needed to.

"What is it?" the professor asked.

Alden looked at me. I took pity on him and said when he was reluctant to.

"Alden received his first two names as a Grim."

Briggs' eyebrows rose in surprise. He looked from me to Alden. "Congratulations. You're a bit young for that, aren't you?"

Alden nodded without looking at him. "Some-sometimes it happens under special circumstances."

Briggs gave him a searching look as if confused by the Grim's reluctance. "What circumstances?"

Alden lifted his hand and allowed the sleeve to fall back from his arm. Silence filled the clearing at the sight of the names written there in blue light.

"I see," Professor Briggs said at last, his voice tight.

He and Mezania looked at each other for a long moment. It felt as though they couldn't get enough of seeing each other. Dara's hand slipped into mine. A drop of water landed on my hand. I looked over to see tears sliding down her cheeks. The tears I had kept at bay spilled over at the sight. I pulled her to me and wrapped my arms around her.

Tears that matched Mezania's trickled down the professor's face. When Briggs nodded, it was clear the motion took a great effort.

"It's time for you to go," he said, his voice breaking.

"I don't want to go," Mezania replied. "I want to stay here with you."

Briggs shook his head and gave her a smile of such tenderness I heard Dara stifle a sob. "This isn't a good life for you, darling," he told her. "You can't be happy staying here like this."

Mezania let out a shuddering breath and lifted her hand to Briggs' cheek. I thought it would pass through the way it did whenever she tried to touch him, but this time, her hand rested just below the scar that marred his face. She gasped. "Trace?"

Briggs glanced at Alden questioningly.

The little Grim lifted his shoulders with a smile on his damp face. "It's the least I can do," he said.

Mezania threw herself into Briggs' arms. He held her close and smoothed her hair down her back. She clung to him as if she would never let him go.

Professor Briggs met Alden's gaze and mouthed, 'Thank you.'

Alden nodded.

Briggs spoke with his lips brushing Mezania's hair. "Remember me the way I was when we were young," he told her.

Mezania shook her head and smiled despite her tears. "I'll remember you as you are now, brave, strong, and the kind of boy I would have loved to live my entire life with. I'm so glad I got this time with you," she told him. When she finally stepped back, she did so with a smile. "I love you, Trace Briggs. I always will."

Briggs returned her loving smile. "I love you, Mezania Brown. I always have and I always will."

Mezania touched his cheek one last time, then turned to Alden. "I'm ready."

Alden held out his hand. The ghost looked at each of us in turn. When her eyes met mine, I said, "Thank you so much for all of your help. I'll always value your friendship."

"And I, yours," she replied. She gave a small laugh. "You helped me overcome my fear of werewolves."

"I'm glad," I replied.

"And I appreciate our talks," Dara said from my side. Her voice broke slightly when she said, "I'm going to miss having you here."

If Briggs was as surprised at the revelation that Mezania and Dara were friends as I was, he didn't show it.

Mezania gave Dara a warm smile. "I'll miss you, too. Keep an eye on Finn. He's a bit reckless."

I rolled my eyes and everyone laughed.

"It's time," Alden said gently.

Mezania slipped her hand into his. Alden whispered a word in a language I didn't know and the name on his wrist grew so bright we had to turned away. When we looked back, they were gone. Briggs let out a stifled sob and leaned against a nearby grave marker. Dara made her way to his side.

Movement caught my eye. I turned to see Sparrow watching us from the top of Mezania's tombstone. She swished her little ghost tail and flapped her wings as if she, too, was ready to go. To my surprise, she looked right at me instead of past us like before. I wondered if it was another gift from Alden, letting us see each other so I could say goodbye.

I knelt on the grass beside where she sat on Mezania's tombstone. "You've been such a great friend," I told the little dragon. "I don't know what I'm going to do without you." I held up my bandaged wrist and tried to force my tone to be light, but I failed entirely when I said, "I miss carrying you around with me."

The little dragon let out a puff of blue flame, but it disappeared in the sunlight. I gave her a watery smile. "I'll miss you, too."

Alden appeared where he had left, but without Mezania at his side. The young Grim gave Professor Briggs a reassuring smile. "She is where she needs to be now, and she is surrounded by loved ones you would know."

His words sent fresh tears trailing from the professor's eyes, but he nodded and set a hand on Alden's shoulder. "Thank you, Alden Grim. You've been a true friend."

Alden sucked in a breath and turned to me. "Are you ready for me to take Sparrow?"

I nodded even though it was a lie. The thought of seeing the little dragon leave the way Mezania had killed me. She had only begun her life, just to sacrifice it to save me. It didn't feel fair.

Alden set his hand on the tombstone with his palm up. The little dragon crossed to it and sat on his hand. Alden closed his eyes and whispered the word in the language I didn't recognize. Instead of vanishing like I expected him to, nothing happened. Alden opened one eye, peaked at me, then closed it and said the word again. Nothing happened.

"That's strange," the Grim said.

I followed his gaze to the name left on his arm. Instead of glowing blue, Sparrow's name brightened and then dimmed over and over.

"What does that mean?" Dara asked.

Alden's eyebrows pulled together. "It means she has a choice."

I stared at him. "What?"

Alden nodded. "It's unique and I've only heard of it one other time in regard to a phoenix, but I don't think Sparrow was supposed to die. The Demon Knight shouldn't have killed her." He stared at me. "I think she gets to decide whether to stay or go!" He lifted his hand to me.

I held out my hand and the little glowing dragon crossed onto it. She sat in the middle of my palm and looked at me with her expectant expression.

I took a steadying breath. "Sparrow, you sacrificed yourself to save me," I told her. I blinked back tears that I refused to let fall. "You don't have to be here anymore if you don't want to." My voice caught. "But I want you here if you want to stay. I-I would really like you here. You deserve to live a good life."

The little dragon's head tipped to the side as she listened to me. I wasn't sure how much she understood, but when her little red tongue snaked out to lick her nose, I couldn't help smiling. The black and purple dragon rose to her feet and tipped her head in the other direction. She opened her mouth. A blue flame came out and washed over my face. I closed my eyes as the mint scent surrounded me. When I opened them again, her ghostly outline had vanished to leave her standing as real and fully formed as if she had never confronted the Demon Knight's flame.

"Look at that!" Dara said.

I looked at my wrist. On it, inscribed in blue glowing light, was Sparrow's name. As we watched, the light faded to leave the word written in scrolling blue letters across the base of my wrist where she liked to sleep.

"She's bound herself to you," Professor Briggs said in amazement. "I didn't know that could happen."

"Neither did I!" Alden replied.

I glanced at his arm, but her name was gone. As if pleased by what had happened, Sparrow flew up my arm and perched on my shoulder. It felt as though she had never left. I turned back to the Academy. My heart felt as though it would burst with happiness as I made my way back to Haunted High with the professor, Dara, and Alden following close behind.

Chapter Fifteen

"MOM, DAD, WHAT ARE you doing here?" Alden asked when we walked into the corridor.

"We're helping with the ghosts, dear. We woke up with a plethora of names and knew we had to come back," his mother explained.

"They're ready to go home now," Mr. Grim said. "I don't know why now is any different than earlier, but they're ready."

We all exchanged glances.

Alden smiled at his dad. "I'm glad it's working now. Can I come with you? I had my first names today. I think I can help."

His father nodded with a proud look on his face. "Of course, son. Let's start upstairs."

I paused at the base of the steps. It didn't feel right to follow them up. I turned to find Vicken holding a cup of water.

"Drink this," he said.

I took it with the realization that I was very thirsty again. When I downed it in a single gulp, he gave me a wry smile that showed his fangs. "I figure you know now how I felt when we got out of that river. I owe you."

I shook my head. "You don't owe me anything. You saved my life and I just did what I could."

His eyes narrowed. "Finn, you let me drink your blood. As messed up as that is, it's far beyond pulling someone up from a river. Also," his voice lowered, "You helped me find Amryn. You upheld your promise. I won't antagonize you anymore. I'm done. I promise."

I brushed it off. "You weren't that bad."

Vicken gave me a straight look. "My coven almost killed you on my orders."

I lifted a shoulder. "Maybe you have too much power."

He grinned. "This coming from an Alpha wolf?"

I laughed. "I'm just saying, killing on command is a little messed up. You need to lighten up on the brainwashing a bit."

Vicken's smile said he didn't take it personally. Then his expression faded to one that was more serious. "I'm going to go check on Amryn. She's resting in my bed until my dad gets here, but I know she's nervous to be alone."

"That's a good idea," I replied.

I watched him climb up the stairs, then followed my stomach to the cafeteria.

"You hungry?" I asked Sparrow. "I imagine coming back to life has to give you quite an appetite." The little dragon's tail lashed back and forth in answer. I dug through the refrigerator until I found a bowl of spaghetti left over from the day before. I held it up for Sparrow to see. "Do dragons like spaghetti?"

She tipped her head at me and blinked her green eyes.

"Worth a try, I guess," I told her. "Bugs are going to get scarce around here the colder it gets. Maybe we need to branch out."

I carried the bowl to the microwave and put it inside. I had just sat down to eat the leftovers when I heard Alden calling my name.

I held up a strand of spaghetti to Sparrow. To my surprise, the dragon grabbed it from my fingers so fast I barely saw it. She slurped the noodle down, then flapped her wings for more.

I grinned at her. "At least one of us can eat."

I carried the bowl with me to the hall.

"Finn, there you are!" Alden said. "I know you can always find me in the kitchen, but you're another story. I never know where to find you! I've been all over this school from the thirteenth floor to the basement."

"Sorry," I told him. "We were hungry."

I glanced at Sparrow and saw that her face was covered in spaghetti sauce. She licked her snout with her forked tongue, cleaning it effectively.

"Come on," Alden said. "We're going to miss it."

The urgency in his voice caught my attention. "Miss what," I asked as I followed him up the stairs.

"You'll see," he said elusively.

As he climbed up the flights, he pulled on the banister to go faster. I glanced over and saw the end of a name on his arm.

"Alden, does your arm say 'Briscoe'?"

He gave me a searching look but continued up without replying. The Grim slowed so that I reached the thirteenth floor ahead of him. I wondered if he was tired, then the sight in front of me told me what was really going on.

"Hello, Finn," Mrs. Grim said.

Mr. Grim inclined his head in welcome.

They stepped aside to reveal the ghost they had been talking to. I found myself face to face with the ghost of my mother once more.

Two thoughts warred in my mind. I feared first that it was merely her memory I saw again and worried she would repeat the saying on how to get to the clubhouse and then disappear as she had before. My other thought argued that she was the demon from the Otherworld, that she was possessed and that she was dangerous to anyone inside Haunted High.

"Hello, Finnley."

Her warm, motherly tone chased all doubt from my mind. I walked forward until I stood between the two Grims.

"H-how is this possible?" I asked them. My gaze never left my mother.

The Grims exchanged a smile. "Sometimes, we get miracles, Finnley. They're little gifts, a chance to say goodbye to those we care about before they move on."

"This is your chance," Alden said from behind me.

His parents stepped back to give us some privacy. At Alden's offer, I handed him the bowl of spaghetti. Sparrow was happy to fly over and join him in eating it. She had apparently found something she enjoyed more than flies and moths.

I turned back to Mom. I didn't know how much time I had, but I wanted to make it count.

"Mom, I'm trying so hard," I began. My throat tightened and I couldn't speak.

She set a hand on my cheek. I covered her hand with mine, happy that I could feel her touch.

"I'm so proud of you, Finnley," she said. "You're doing so much good here." Tears showed in her eyes, but she smiled. "I'm so glad I got to see the young man you've become."

"I'm so glad I got to see you," I replied. "I didn't think it was possible."

Her smile was warm when she said, "Anything is possible for you, Finnley. You are pure and good and mean well in what you do." Her smile touched her eyes when she said, "Just try to take care of yourself, alright?"

I nodded. "I will, Mom."

"It's time," Mr. Grim said from behind me.

My mother gave me one last smile and then nodded at the Grim. "I'm ready."

Alden stepped forward with his parents and Sparrow returned to my shoulder. I fought back tears as the Grims circled my mom. She watched me with a warm smile on her face until the name on Alden's wrist grew so bright that I had to shut my eyes. Silvia Roe Briscoe's name remained bright in my retinas with my eyes closed. When I opened them, the Grims and my mother had gone.

Peace filled me. As hard as it had been to watch her go, I knew she was where she needed to be. And for some reason, she was proud of me. The smile wouldn't leave my face when I walked back down to my dorm room. I felt as though I wanted to cry and laugh at the same time. I settled for falling onto my bed. I was asleep before I could even think to take off my shoes.

The next morning felt disappointingly uneventful as I sat through Professor Seedly's discourse on the difference between petal veins and leaf veins during Care of Green Multicellular Organisms. One of the students whispered 'plant' and nearly got himself kicked out. Even Sparrow wearied of sitting on my shoulder and flitted between the shrubbery that covered the room from floor to ceiling in search of bugs. Alden made bets with the sphinx girl who sat next to him on whether the sylph dragon would catch a fly or a spider.

I tossed my books onto my desk in History of Witches and Warlocks and flipped my notebook open to an empty page before I realized something was different. I looked at the paper and noticed that I could see the lines too clearly. I glanced up at the lights overhead. The faint hum of the neon lights sounded strange to my ears even though I heard them in every other classroom. But the candles weren't lit and the lights were on. I heard other students whispering about how strange it was as they entered the room and took their seats.

Headmistress Wrengold arrived at the door after the bell rang.

"Where's Professor Briggs?" I asked before she could address the class.

She gave me a small smile. "He had to go away for a while. I am just here to introduce Professor Gertrude, your substitute until Professor Briggs returns."

A woman with short blonde hair and green cat eyes entered. She smiled at the students with a hint of nervousness on her face.

"I am honored to be here—" she began.

I rose from my seat. "Can I be excused?"

"Mr. Briscoe, that's not polite," the Headmistress told me.

I looked around. Everyone was watching me. Aerlis, the boy with orange horns, stuck out his tongue and then grinned.

"I, uh," I searched for an excuse. "I've got to use the bathroom."

"You better let him, Headmistress Wrengold," Aerlis said, coming to my rescue in his crude way. "I've heard werewolves can make quite the mess."

Laughter flooded the room, but I didn't even care. If it helped me leave, I was grateful for it.

"Yes, well, go ahead, Mr. Briscoe," the Headmistress replied in a flustered tone.

I left my books on the desk and rushed out the door. "Sorry Professor Gertrude," I called behind me. "It's nice to meet you!"

I ran down to the main corridor and slipped behind the huge unicorn photograph. Taking the stairs four and five at a time, I burst through the door into the basement. No one was there. I ran to Mercer's box in the far corner and threw the lid open. The small box with the piece of Chutka's heart was gone. In its place, a small, folded piece of paper waited. The name 'Mercer' was written on the front in Professor Briggs' elegant handwriting.

I opened the letter and read quickly.

Finn, you really shouldn't read a note left for someone else, but since I suspect you're the one who found this, I want you to relay a message to Mercer. Let him know that the Wiccan Enforcer is in our world. She is searching for the piece of heart in the box. I've taken it far enough away to save the Academy from retaliation, but we both know she'll have my trail before long. Find me at 40.730610 and -73.935242.

Briggs

Trepidation filled me as I ran back up the stairs to the infirmary. For Professor Briggs to leave his classes and the school, the threat the Wiccan Enforcer posed must be serious.

"He knows you can't follow him," I said as soon as Mercer finished the letter and set it down.

"I would," he replied. "But I think Dr. Six would shoot me herself if I tried to get out of this bed."

"I'm going."

"That's a bad idea," the sweeper told me, his dark stone face expressionless despite the pain of his wounds.

"Somebody has to help him. We both know Briggs wouldn't have left a message if he was alright."

Mercer had to acknowledge my reasoning. He looked at the note again, then said, "Maybe he meant for it to be found later."

"He knew I'd find it when he didn't show up to teach second period."

Mercer gave the first chuckle I had ever heard from him. "He knows you're a stubborn snoop."

I stared at him.

The sweeper met my gaze, his laughter gone as if it had never happened. "But you're a good kid and you put together a good team. They'll take care of this school while you're gone."

"I can go?" I said in surprise.

"You will whether I allow it or not," Mercer replied. "I'd tie you up or something creative, but since I'm confined to this bed, I doubt you'll let me get close enough."

I hid a grin as I backed away. "Not a chance."

Mercer nodded. "Take care of yourself and grab the black box on the table before you leave."

"What table?" I asked.

"The table in the basement," he replied.

"It was empty when I went down there."

"It's not empty anymore," he said.

I was shocked when I hurried back to the basement and really did find a black box in the middle of the table. I grabbed it and jogged back up the stairs to the main corridor, then out from the picture frame and up the stairs to my room.

"We really need fewer stairs in this place," I muttered. I shoved a few belongings into my backpack along with the box.

"Where are you going."

I paused at Vicken's voice. I turned to face him in the doorway.

"Uh, class," I said. I cringed at the sound of the lie in my voice.

"Isn't werewolves being horrible liars a bit cliché?" the vampire asked.

"You mean like stealthy, sneaky vampires who snoop around in someone else's business is cliché?" I shot back.

He gave me a toothy grin. "Where are you going, Finn?"

I sighed and admitted, "I'm leaving to find Briggs. He left a note for Mercer. Mercer can't go."

"So you're filling in. Does Mercer know?"

"He didn't try to stop me."

Vicken rolled his eyes. "He's confined to a bed. Of course he didn't try to stop you."

"He gave me a box to take."

Vicken's dark eyebrows lifted. "I'll get my backpack."

"Where are we going?"

I sighed at the sound of Alden's voice. He came into the room with an innocent, inquiring expression on his face.

"Nowhere. You need to stay and cover for us."

"No way," the Grim replied. "I know that expression on your face. It says you're about to do something dangerous and you need someone to watch out for you."

I glanced in the mirror hung crookedly above the desk in our room. "It doesn't say that."

"It does," Vicken called from the doorway as he left for his room.

I sighed. "Fine, but I can't guarantee your safety."

Alden laughed. "What is this, some spy movie? This is life, Finn, and in life, you're going to have to accept that you have friends that have your back whether you like it or not."

"Why wouldn't I like having friends that have my back?" I asked.

"Why were you going to leave alone?" Alden shot back as he threw a change of clothes into a satchel.

I sucked in a breath to reply, then realized I didn't have anything to say. I grimaced and went with, "You know me too well. It's scary."

"That's the problem with roommates," Alden said.

I rolled my eyes and headed for the stairs. "I'll meet you by the front door."

"If you leave, I'll just follow," he called out.

Grumbling about friends who couldn't leave well enough alone, I hitched my backpack up higher and made my way for the front entrance.

I had just reached the main corridor when someone called out, "Finn, wait!"

I closed my eyes for a moment, took a calming breath, and turned with the thought that I had made too many friends at Haunted High.

"If I bring anyone else, Mercer, Briggs, and the Headmistress will have my hide," I said to Dara.

She stifled a smile when she said, "I wasn't asking to go with you anywhere."

Caught off-guard, I admitted, "You're right. I jumped to conclusions."

She stopped a few steps away and said, "I just want to make sure you're alright."

"Me?" I thought about everything that had happened; my thoughts lingered on saying goodbye to my mother. As hard as the last few days had been, I knew my answer. "I'm fine," I told her.

"Really?" she asked.

I nodded. "Really. Thanks to your help with the Demon Knight, I still have my hands." I held them out and grimaced at the sight of my still-healing palm. "At least as good as they are."

"Alden told me about Sparrow," she said. She smiled at the sleeping dragon and stepped forward to run a finger down her back. "I'm so happy for you."

I smiled, too. "I got lucky on that one."

"We all did," she replied.

I watched her pet the little dragon and realized that I was about to do again what I had promised not to, I was going to lead Sparrow into danger I wasn't sure I could protect her from. The world outside of the Academy wasn't a place for a baby dragon. Vicken, Alden, and I might blend in with some effort and a whole lot of luck, but the dragon around my wrist would be a danger to us all, and especially to her.

"I have a favor to ask you," I told Dara.

She gave me a surprised look. "Anything."

I lifted my wrist. "Would you look after Sparrow? I'm pretty sure where we're going is dangerous, and I refuse to put her at risk again."

Dara looked taken aback by my request, but she nodded. "I would be honored to take care of her, Finn."

"Thank you," I replied. I ran a finger down Sparrow's back. "Hey little one, can you wake up for a minute?"

The dragon raised her head and gave me a sleepy look.

I turned my wrist so she could see Dara. "I'm going somewhere you can't go. Dara says she'll take good care of you and make sure you're safe while I'm gone. Is that alright?"

The dragon looked from me to Dara. At first, I thought she would refuse, but then the sylph dragon rose, stretched, and padded onto Dara's outstretched hand. Dara's violet eyes were wide as the dragon curled herself around the empath's slender wrist and went back to sleep.

At Dara's shocked look, I lifted a shoulder. "Professor Seedly mentioned that dragons don't do well when they're left by the one they've chosen to protect them, but I figure an empath can help her feel safe and loved. She knows I wouldn't choose someone who would do a bad job, and she can feel that you'll protect her." Uncertainty filled me and I gave her a worried look. "Is that alright?"

She nodded. "More than alright. I'm honored, Finn. I can't believe you trust me this much."

The surprise on her face made me smile. I pushed a strand of hair back from her cheek just for the excuse to touch her. She leaned closer. My eyes drifted to her lips as the voice in the back of my mind whispered that it would be nice to kiss her again. I lowered my head to meet her lifted face.

"Hey, you love birds going to talk all day or are we going on an adventure?" Vicken asked.

His voice shattered the moment as effectively as if he had thrown a bomb into the room. Dara and I backed quickly away from each other. Her cheeks burned red with the same embarrassment I knew colored mine.

"This school has very strict policies about public displays of affection," the vampire continued with enjoyment at our embarrassment. He passed us with a lazy wink of one yellow eye. "Even if you are a werewolf."

I let out a frustrated breath and met Dara's gaze. She gave me a smile that made her violet eyes sparkle.

"Don't be gone too long," she said.

"I won't," I promised.

Alden reached the bottom of the stairs and crossed to us.

"You won't what? Is Dara coming?"

I rolled my eyes at Dara's answering laughter and turned toward the door.

"Ignore them," Vicken advised the Grim. "They're mushy."

"Someday you might actually like girls, Vicken," Dara told him. "Just hope that you haven't ostracized yourself from anyone who might like you back."

"Oh, you like me," Vicken told her. He paused with his hand on the door. "Don't you?"

When she just laughed and turned away, Vicken asked me, "Girls like me, don't they?"

"Sure," I replied. "Everyone likes cold, hostile, angry vampire types."

He nodded. "Yes, they do."

I led the way out the door. It closed behind us with a slam of finality.

"What was that?" Alden asked.

I glanced back. "It always does that."

"I've never seen it do that," Vicken said, eyeing the door.

I shrugged. "The school is haunted. I thought everyone knew that. Isn't that why it's called Haunted High?"

"I thought it was a joke," Alden said. He hitched his backpack up higher and ran down the stairs after us. "Wait up you guys!"

"Where are we going?" Vicken asked.

My wrist gave a warm throb where Sparrow's name was written in blue scrolling letters. I already missed the dragon. To distract myself, I pulled out the note and opened it so that the vampire could see what Professor Briggs had written. "To these coordinates," I said. When he paused, I glanced at him. "Is something wrong? That's where we're supposed to meet the professor."

206

Vicken shook his head and said, "If I'm not mistaken, which I'm not, that's the Mythic Labs. We have a serious problem."

"Mythic Labs?" I repeated. "As in labs where mythics do experiments? That doesn't sound so bad."

Vicken and Alden both looked worried when Vicken replied, "No. It's the labs where they experiment on mythics. Briggs is in trouble."

About the Author

Cheree Alsop is an award-winning, best-selling author who has published over 40 books. She is the mother of a beautiful, talented daughter and amazing twin sons who fill every day with joy and laughter. She is married to her best friend, Michael, the light of her life and her soulmate who shares her dreams and inspires her by reading the first drafts and giving much appreciated critiques. Cheree works as a fulltime author and mother, which is more play than work! She enjoys reading, traveling to tropical beaches, riding motorcycles, spending time with her wonderful children, and going on family adventures while planning her next book.

Cheree and Michael live in Utah where they rock out, enjoy the outdoors, plan great quests, and never stop dreaming.

Look for updates on the rest of the books from this series on Cheree's website. You can also find information on Cheree's other books at www.chereealsop.com

To be added to Cheree's email list for notification of book releases, please send her an email to chereelalsop@hotmail.com

If you enjoyed this book, please review it so that others will be able to share in the adventure!

REVIEWS

The Girl from the Stars Series

This is my favorite Cheree Alsop book now! Her best yet! I loved it. So many twists and turns, great characters, excitement and hints of romance. I can't wait for the next one in the series.
—Voca Matisse, Reviewer

Fantastic book! Cheree's ability to write an amazing character that you not only sympathize with but also grow to care for, is one of the fabulous writing abilities that she lends to every story. This story line was full of epic twists and wry humor that had me engaged the entire way through. All in all a fun enjoyable read.
—akgodwin, Amazon Reviewer

This was one of the best books I have read in a while. Sci-fi, adventure, thriller... could not put the book away. I already bought the second book in the series, and hope the third will come out soon.
—Kindle Customer

The main character, Liora, is a very mixed up but emerging person who is a genetic mutt! Half of her DNA is totally violence oriented whilst the other half is straight human, which is to say violent when necessary but basically well rounded. In the beginning she was a slave in a circus and had never known anyone she could trust or care for, and even when she is rescued from that hell she has a hard time adjusting to the idea that she can fit in anywhere. The action is frequent and well written and over time she keeps trying to both find reasons to fit in and reasons to strike out on her own. This is not resolved in the first book, and makes you want to read more. I like the series a lot and hope the writer keeps them coming.

—Sam, Amazon Reviewer

Dr Wolf, the Fae Rift Series

Dr. Wolf, the Fae Rift Series Book 1- Shockwave by Cheree Alsop is a movie transcript ready and suspensefully alluring tale that weaves the mind of the reader around the world of wild dreams.

— Rachel Anderson, Amazon Reviewer

Wow! Was not expecting enjoying this book as much as I did. Ms. Alsop had me drawn in front the get go. The writing was fantastic, the story just flowed so easily and I could not put the book down. I enjoyed all the characters and love her imagination. The banter with the characters had me laughing out loud (I love the fairy and the vampire). I really enjoyed the storyline and the whole what if of falling into a rift. I would highly recommend this book to anyone looking for a nice fresh look on paranormal.

— Amazon Verified Reviewer

Demon Spiral picks up right where Shockwave left off...Once again, I could not put this book down. The flow of the story is amazing and the banter that the author was able to put into the book just made for a very enjoyable read. I highly recommend Cheree Alsop and look forward to reading the next in this series as well.

—Crystal's Review, GoodReads Reviewer

I had to download the sample for this because I was sure I wanted it. I bought the book after the first page. It's almost like Dr. Who with Fae.

—Chris Hughes, Amazon Reviewer

The Silver Series

"Cheree Alsop has written *Silver* for the YA reader who enjoys both werewolves and coming-of-age tales. Although I don't fall into this demographic, I still found it an entertaining read on a long plane trip! The author has put a great deal of thought into balancing a tale that could apply to any teen (death of a parent, new school, trying to find one's place in the world) with the added spice of a youngster dealing with being exceptionally different from those around him, and knowing that puts him in danger."

—Robin Hobb, author of the Farseer Trilogy

"I honestly am amazed this isn't absolutely EVERYWHERE! Amazing book. Could NOT put it down! After reading this book, I purchased the entire series!"

—Josephine, Amazon Reviewer

"A page-turner that kept me wide awake and wanting more. Great characters, well written, tenderly developed, and thrilling. I loved this book, and you will too."

—Valerie McGilvrey

"Super glad that I found this series! I am crushed that it is at its end. I am sure we will see some of the characters in the next series, but it just won't be the same. I am 41 years old, and am only a little embarrassed to say I was crying at 3 a.m. this morning while finishing the last book. Although this is a YA series, all ages will enjoy the Silver Series. Great job by

Cheree Alsop. I am excited to see what she comes up with next."

—Jennc, Amazon Reviewer

The Werewolf Academy Series

If you love werewolves, paranormal, and looking for a book like House of Night or Vampire Academy this is it! YA for sure.

—Reviewer for Sweets Books

I got this book from a giveaway, and it's one of the coolest books I have ever read. If you love Hogwarts, and Vampire Academy, or basically anything that has got to do with supernatural people studying, this is the book for you.

—Maryam Dinzly

This series is truly a work of art, sucked in immediately and permanently. The first line and you are in the book. Cheree Alsop is a gifted writer, all of her books are my complete favorites!! This series has to be my absolute favorite, Alex is truly a wonderful character who I so wish was real so I can meet him and thank him. Once you pick this book up you won't put it down till it's finished. A must read!!!!!

—BookWolf Brianna

Listed with Silver Moon as the top most emotional of Cheree's books, I loved Instinct for its raw truth about the pain, the heartbreak, and the guilt that Alex fights.

—Loren Weaver

Great story. Loaded with adventure at every turn. Can't wait till the next book. Very enjoyable, light reading. I would recommend to all young and old readers.

—Sharon Klein

The Galdoni Series

"This is absolutely one of the best books I have ever read in my life! I loved the characters and their personalities, the storyline and the way it was written. The bravery, courage and sacrifice that Kale showed was amazing and had me scolding myself to get a grip and stop crying! This book had adventure, romance and comedy all rolled into one terrific book I LOVED the lesson in this book, the struggles that the characters had to go through (especially the forbidden love)...I couldn't help wondering what it would be like to live among such strangely beautiful creatures that acted, at times, more caring and compassionate than the humans. Overall, I loved this book...I recommend it to ANYONE who fancies great books."

—iBook Reviewer

"I was not expecting a free novel to beat anything that I have ever laid eyes upon. This book was touching and made me want more after each sentence."

— Sears1994, iBook Reviewer

"This book was simply heart wrenching. It was an amazing book with a great plot. I almost cried several times. All of the scenes were so real it felt like I was there witnessing everything."

—Jeanine Drake, iBook Reveiwer

"Galdoni is an amazing book; it is the first to actually make me cry! It is a book that really touches your heart, a romance novel that might change the way you look at someone. It did that to me."
—Coralee2, Reviewer

"Wow. I simply have no words for this. I highly recommend it to anyone who stumbled across this masterpiece. In other words, READ IT!"
—Troublecat101, iBook Reviewer

The Monster Asylum Series

What a rollercoaster, wow!! I never ever cried when reading a vampire book, but I did this time. I must say it's the best vampire book I've read since ever. One of the best books ever read so far.
—Conny, Goodreads Reviewer

I downloaded this book because of Cheree, I love her imagination. This one is so much fun to read; once I started I couldn't put it down. And now I believe not all Monsters are bad!! Looking forward to the next book in the series. Thanks Cheree
—Doughgirl61, Amazon Reviewer

Keeper of the Wolves

"This is without a doubt the VERY BEST paranormal romance/adventure I have ever read and I've been reading these types of books for over 45 years. Excellent plot, wonderful protagonists—even the evil villains were great. I

read this in one sitting on a Saturday morning when there were so many other things I should have been doing. I COULD NOT put it down! I also appreciated the author's research and insights into the behavior of wolf packs. I will CERTAINLY read more by this author and put her on my 'favorites' list."
—N. Darisse

"This is a novel that will emotionally cripple you. Be sure to keep a box of tissues by your side. You will laugh, you will cry, and you will fall in love with Keeper. If you loved *Black Beauty* as a child, then you will truly love *Keeper of the Wolves* as an adult. Put this on your 'must read' list."
—Fortune Ringquist

"Cheree Alsop mastered the mind of a wolf and wrote the most amazing story I've read this year. Once I started, I couldn't stop reading. Personal needs no longer existed. I turned the last page with tears streaming down my face."
—Rachel Andersen, Amazon Reviewer

"I just finished this book. Oh my goodness, did I get emotional in some spots. It was so good. The courage and love portrayed is amazing. I do recommend this book. Thought provoking."
—Candy, Amazon Reviewer

Thief Prince

"I absolutely loved this book! I could not put it down. . . The Thief Prince will whisk you away into a new world that you will not want to leave! I hope that Ms. Alsop has more about this story to write, because I would love more Kit and

Andric! This is one of my favorite books so far this year! Five Stars!"
—Crystal, Book Blogger at Books are Sanity

". . . Once I started I couldn't put it down. The story is amazing. The plot is new and the action never stops. The characters are believable and the emotions presented are beautiful and real. If anyone wants a good, clean, fun, romantic read, look no further. I hope there will be more books set in Debria, or better yet, Antor."
—SH Writer, Amazon Reviewer

"This book was a roller coaster of emotions: tears, laughter, anger, and happiness. I absolutely fell in love with all of the characters placed throughout this story. This author knows how to paint a picture with words."
—Kathleen Vales

"Awesome book! It was so action packed, I could not put it down, and it left me wanting more! It was very well written, leaving me feeling like I had a connection with the characters."
—M. A., Amazon Reviewer

The Shadows Series

"This was a heart-warming tale of rags to riches. It was also wonderfully described and the characters were vivid and vibrant; a story that teaches of love defying boundaries and of people finding acceptance."
—Sara Phillip, Book Reviewer

"This is the best book I have ever had the pleasure of reading. . . It literally has everything, drama, action, fighting, romance, adventure, & suspense. . . Nexa is one of the most incredible female protagonists ever written. . .It literally had me on pins & needles the ENTIRE time. . . I cannot recommend this book highly enough. Please give yourself a wonderful treat & read this book... you will NOT be disappointed!!!"

—Jess- Goodreads Reviewer

"Took my breath away; excitement, adventure and suspense. . . This author has extracted a tender subject and created a supernatural fantasy about seeing beyond the surface of an individual. . . Also the romantic scenes would make a girl swoon. . . The fights between allies and foes and blood lust would attract the male readers. . .The conclusion was so powerful and scary this reader was sitting on the edge of her seat."

—Susan Mahoney, Book Blogger

"Adventure, incredible amounts of imagination and description go into this world! It is a buy now, don't leave the couch until the last chapter has reached an end kind of read!"

—Malcay- Amazon Reviewer

"The high action tale with the underlying love story that unfolds makes you want to keep reading and not put it down. I can't wait until the next book in the Shadows Series comes out."

—Karen- Amazon Reviewer

". . . It's refreshing to see a female character portrayed without the girly clichés most writers fall into. She is someone I would like to meet in real life, and it is nice to read the first person POV of a character who is so well-round that she is brave, but still has the softer feminine side that defines her character. A definite must read."

—S. Teppen- Goodreads Reviewer

The Small Town Superhero Series

"A very human superhero- Cheree Alsop has written a great book for youth and adults alike. Kelson, the superhero, is battling his own demons plus bullies in this action packed narrative. Small Town Superhero had me from the first sentence through the end. I felt every sorrow, every pain and the delight of rushing through the dark on a motorcycle. Descriptions in Small Town Superhero are so well written the reader is immersed in the town and lives of its inhabitants."

—Rachel Andersen, Book Reviewer

"Anyone who grew up in a small town or around motorcycles will love this! It has great characters and flows well with martial arts fighting and conflicts involved."

—Karen, Amazon Reviewer

"Fantastic story...and I love motorcycles and heroes who don't like the limelight. Excellent character development. You'll like this series!"

—Michael, Amazon Reviewer

"Another great read; couldn't put it down. Would definitely recommend this book to friends and family. She has put out another great read. Looking forward to reading more!"

—Benton Garrison, Amazon Reviewer

"I enjoyed this book a lot. Good teen reading. Most books I read are adult contemporary; I needed a change and this was a good change. I do recommend reading this book! I will be looking out for more books from this author. Thank you!"

—Cass, Amazon Reviewer

Stolen

"This book will take your heart, make it a little bit bigger, and then fill it with love. I would recommend this book to anyone from 10-100. To put this book in words is like trying to describe love. I had just gotten it and I finished it the next day because I couldn't put it down. If you like action, thrilling fights, and/or romance, then this is the perfect book for you."

—Steven L. Jagerhorn

"Couldn't put this one down! Love Cheree's ability to create totally relatable characters and a story told so fluidly you actually believe it's real."

—Sue McMillin, Amazon Reviewer

"I enjoyed this book it was exciting and kept you interested. The characters were believable. And the teen romance was cute."

—Book Haven- Amazon Reviewer

"I really liked this book . . . I was pleasantly surprised to discover this well-written book. . .I'm looking forward to reading more from this author."

—Julie M. Peterson- Amazon Reviewer

"Great book! I enjoyed this book very much it keeps you wanting to know more! I couldn't put it down! Great read!"
—Meghan- Amazon Reviewer

"A great read with believable characters that hook you instantly. . . I was left wanting to read more when the book was finished."
—Katie- Goodreads Reviewer

Heart of the Wolf

"Absolutely breathtaking! This book is a roller coaster of emotions that will leave you exhausted!!! A beautiful fantasy filled with action and love. I recommend this book to all fantasy lovers and those who enjoy a heartbreaking love story that rivals that of Romeo and Juliet. I couldn't put this book down!"
—Amy May

"What an awesome book! A continual adventure, with surprises on every page. What a gifted author she is. You just can't put the book down. I read it in two days. Cheree has a way of developing relationships and pulling at your heart. You find yourself identifying with the characters in her book...True life situations make this book come alive for you and gives you increased understanding of your own situation in life. Magnificent story and characters. I've read all of Cheree's books and recommend them all to you...especially if you love adventures."
—Michael, Amazon Reviewer

"You'll like this one and want to start part two as soon as you can! If you are in the mood for an adventure book in a

faraway kingdom where there are rival kingdoms plotting and scheming to gain more power, you'll enjoy this novel. The characters are well developed, and of course with Cheree there is always a unique supernatural twist thrown into the story as well as romantic interests to make the pages fly by."
Karen, Amazon Reviewer

When Death Loved an Angel

"This style of book is quite a change for this author so I wasn't expecting this, but I found an interesting story of two very different souls who stepped outside of their "accepted roles" to find love and forgiveness, and what is truly of value in life and death."
—Karen, Amazon Reviewer

"When Death Loved an Angel by Cheree Alsop is a touching paranormal romance that cranks the readers' thinking mode into high gear."
—Rachel Andersen, Book Reviewer

"Loved this book. I would recommend this book to everyone. And be sure to check out the rest of her books, too!"
—Malcay, Book Reviewer

The Million Dollar Gift

...This was a very beautiful, heart warming story about a young man who finds love, and family again on Christmas. I really enjoyed this short story. It truly inspires the meaning of

Christmas in my eyes. It was utterly beautiful, and I highly recommend it. The plot is very interesting, and the characters catch your heart and lead on this very sad and happy story.

—Whitney@Shooting Stars Review

I recommend The Million Dollar Gift as a way to remember what Christmas is about: Love. Family. Friendship. Because a life without love isn't really worth living anyway.

—Loren Weaver

When Chase risks his life to save a brother and sister just before Christmas, his life becomes entwined with theirs more intricately than he could have imagined. Emotional and moving, this is a story of a young man whose troubled heart is tested by the one thing he is unprepared to face, love. MY TAKE- This is a fast, fun, emotional Christmas read. Made me cry.

—Donna Weaver

Never stop dreaming!

CPSIA information can be obtained
at www.ICGtesting.com
Printed in the USA
LVOW03s0521141217
559667LV00001B/25/P